# ORPHAN TRAIN MEMORIES

## RACHEL WESSON

*For my youngest sister, Annie whose brave battle with cancer inspires me on a daily basis. Despite her suffering, her thoughts are always for other people.*

# PROLOGUE

*S*itting in the pew of the small church, clutching her six-year-old son's hand, Kathleen felt thrills of excitement fly down her spine as the music announced the bride's arrival. Kathleen's gaze moved to the groom and the best man, both dressed in formal black suits. She closed her eyes, remembering the first time she'd met Patrick, then an orphan traveling on the same orphan train she'd taken to try to find her brothers, Michael and Shane. Patrick had saved the life of the outplacement agent when her skirt caught fire; he still had the scars on his hands to prove it. Richard, a doctor who happened to be on the train at the time, had looked after Patrick's burns. When she'd married Richard, they formally adopted Patrick.

Little Richie, squirmed on the seat beside her. He and Patrick couldn't be closer than real brothers and both adored their seven-year-old sister, Esme, who was one of Frieda's flower girls. Both youngsters were devastated that Frieda and Patrick were moving to London, as Frieda had been a huge part of their lives.

If not for Frieda's brother Hans saving baby Esme after the General Slocum sank…Kathleen shuddered not wanting to think about that horrible day when so many lost their lives including ten year old Hans.

Kathleen grasped Lily's hand as the bridal party made their way to the front of the church where Father Nelson waited to officiate. Esme walked alongside Coleen Doherty, with Grace and Evie following behind. Frieda looked stunning as she walked, straight-backed like a queen, in her long, beautiful white dress, a veil of Irish lace covering her face. Charlie, accompanying her to the Altar, couldn't have looked prouder if the bride were his own daughter.

Emily, Gustav's wife had managed to produce a small bouquet despite it being so late in the year.

New Year's Eve was a special day to have a wedding, a day to forget the horrors of the year they had just had and look forward to the promises 1912 held. Today she was gaining a daughter, but soon she would wave goodbye to her son and his wife as they headed to London to begin a new life. Patrick as a doctor at the Brompton hospital in Chelsea and Frieda starting her career at the Woman's hospital.

Richard thought they might return to live in America, but Kathleen wasn't too sure. It was difficult for Patrick, despite being a wonderful doctor in his own right, he would always feel he traveled in his father's shadow. Especially as Richard's reputation as a burns specialist had grown since the tragedy of the Triangle Shirtwaist fire. Kathleen's mood dipped thinking of that horrible day. Lily hadn't been the same since the fire, having lost her spark, her determination to change lives for the better. Kathleen's heart ached for Lily and her family. The twins Teddy and Laurie, at seventeen, were absorbed with their own lives. Grace was too young at sixteen to be looking after her younger sisters, Evie and Coleen, Kathleen thought. She shook her head; what was she thinking? She hadn't been much older than Grace when she'd lost her family and met Lily for the first time. But Lily's family had been brought up in a very sheltered environment, totally different from the one Kathleen and her siblings had endured in the tenement and miles from the horror of Lily's childhood.

KATHLEEN WANTED to hug Lily but made do with a squeeze of her hand. Lily and Charlie were going traveling for three months, leaving with the honeymoon couple, but Kathleen knew it would feel longer. She'd spent virtually every day with Lily since they'd met all those years ago. How she would miss her but she hoped the trip would allow Lily to recover. Richard believed a change of scenery and some rest would bring back the Lily she knew and loved from Ireland. In the meantime, minding Lily's five children plus supervising the sanctuary would keep her busy.

The priest's voice broke into Kathleen's thoughts as the ceremony began, the familiar Latin flowing over them. She listened as her son and Frieda repeated their vows, Frieda's voice breaking slightly. Tears fell down Kathleen's cheeks. Lily handed her a hanky as she wiped her own face. What was it about weddings that made people cry?

Kathleen and Lily exchanged a smile as Patrick kissed Frieda chastely under the watchful eyes of the priest. Then they turned to look at their guests. Kathleen had an urge to clap but Father Nelson would have had a heart attack and given his advanced years, that was likely to be fatal.

She couldnt wait to get out of the church and give her son and his wife a big hug. She made her way carefully down the aisle, shivering as she neared the exit, the winter's chilly evening made a little brighter by a flurry of snowflakes.

Kathleen nodded to the many faces she recognized. Smothered giggles caught her attention as Teddy stopped young Richie from grabbing Esme's dress. She watched as Patrick held Frieda's hand leading her down the few

5

steps to the sidewalk outside. Their guests cheered.

"Wasn't it a beautiful wedding? My bladder has never been so near my eyes." Cook's muffled voice flowed across the silence of the church making more than one person smile. Kathleen nodded but wasn't really paying attention as a group of female wedding guests stared at a man approaching her, wearing a full Navy dress uniform. "Aunty Kathleen, you look beautiful," he said.

"Kenny? Is it really you? My goodness, nobody told me you were coming," Kathleen exclaimed, enveloping him in a hug before stepping back.

He held out his arm. "Can I escort you somewhere. We seem to be causing a blockage."

She looked around to find everyone staring at them, well more at him judging by the admiring looks coming from the ladies. She took his arm.

"Wait until Father Nelson sees you."

The wedding reception was held in a hotel. Champagne flowed as the guests, many from the tenements where Kathleen and Frieda had grown up, others from high society such as Mr. Prentice and his wife, Sadie, still more from the hospital where Patrick and Frieda worked, mingled.

"Kenneth Clare, sorry Watson. As I live and breathe it, I'd never have recognised you but for the uniform." Father Nelson shuffled over to where Kathleen and Lily stood with Kenny and the twins. "Please tell me you have leave and spend some time with your old friends."

'Yes Father. I've been transferred to a new ship. Captain gave me two weeks shore leave so I thought I'd drop in to see you all before making my way to Riverside Springs to see mam and dad. Mam's not been too well, with her heart and everything. Dad wrote to say he hopes I can convince her to take things easier."

Father Nelson and Kathleen exchanged a look. "The day anyone makes Bridget Collins, I mean Watson, do something is a day I'd love to see. Since the first time I met your mother, she has never stopped moving."

Kenny nodded in agreement before Laurie interrupted. "Have you seen any of the Naval planes in action? Ever since Ely made the first landing on the USS Pennsylvania, it can only be a matter of time before hundreds follow in his wake. I'd love to be one of them."

Kenny didn't get a chance to answer as Lily said "Mr. Ely died a few weeks ago, Laurie. I don't want you following in his footsteps."

"I don't intend dying! Kenny, want to find Patrick and talk to him about his trip. Maybe you can give him some pointers for his sea voyage."

Kathleen and Lily exchanged an amazed look at the feeble excuse as the boys made their way across the room leaving Father Nelson to comment, "I doubt you will ever put that lad off flying, Lily. He seems to have it in his blood. Sometimes, parents must let their children go and live their own lives, you know."

Taking one look at Lily's face, Kathleen excused them both.

"Apologies Father Nelson but we promised Frieda we would help her change into her other gown. Patrick is taking her off to a secret location for a few days prior to their trip to London. We will be back soon."

Kathleen led Lily through the assembled

guests. "I know you didn't like hearing what Father Nelson said but he might be right. Laurie is dead set on becoming a pilot and the more you try to stop him the more he will want it."

"It's so dangerous, though."

Kathleen patted her friend's arm. "Haven't the events of the last few years shown us how life can be fragile. Better for him to do something he loves doing than spend his life in misery being forced to follow a path not of his choosing."

Lily opened her mouth but Kathleen hastily added. "Let's not discuss it any more tonight. This is a celebration. Let's find Frieda. It's almost time for them to leave."

Frieda changed into a new dress, and the guests assembled to see them off. Kathleen swallowed the lump in her throat and held the tears back as she waved them off. She saw Lily doing the same. Richard offered her his arm. "Are you ready to go home, Mrs. Green?"

"Yes, darling. Didn't they look wonderful together? I think they will be very happy," Kathleen replied.

"If Frieda makes Patrick half as happy as you have made me, he will be a very lucky man," Richard said, leaning in to brush his lips against hers, making her blush like a schoolgirl. She linked arms and let her husband escort her home.

# CHAPTER 1

*L*eonie Chiver forced herself to put her foot on the ground, using the crutches supplied by the hospital. All the doctors believed she should be able to walk again with a stick or crutch to help her. Gritting her teeth, she ignored the pain and pushed herself to her feet. She managed to stand for four or five seconds before falling back into the chair. She almost screamed with frustration. Carrie came running in and stopped when she saw the tears sliding down Leonie's face. She stood near the end of the bed.

"What's wrong? Are you in pain? Should I call Cook?" Carrie hopped from one foot to another.

"No, I'm fine. I was just doing my exercises."

"So you can walk again. Show me." Carrie stared at Leonie's legs as if willing them to move.

Leonie shook her head. "I've done enough for today."

Carrie's face fell, tears glistening in her eyes. "I heard them talking about sending us to Riverside Springs. To Miss Kathleen's sister. They were talking about sending us without you. To give you time to recover." Carrie gave her an accusing stare. "You aren't going to get better, are you? If you really wanted to get better, you would work harder."

Carrie ran before Leonie could contradict her. Who was talking about sending the children away, and why now? She stared over at the window, with the chair situated just beside it. Lily and Kathleen had cleared out a storeroom to give her a bedroom on the ground floor. She could use her wheelchair, but she knew they hoped it would also encourage her to try walking with the crutches. She looked around the room at the finishing touches they had added: the jug and basin on the chest of drawers, the embroidered pretty cover for the bed, the cheerful painting of a girl dancing on the wall. Everything was picked with care to make her feel comfortable.

Sitting on the side of the bed, Leonie pictured her mother, Johanna, remembering all she had done to keep their family together. Johanna hadn't given up, even when ravaged by disease. She'd kept fighting to the very end and had made Leonie promise to keep her family together. Leonie brushed the tears from her eyes. She had to be able to walk, even just a little bit. But could she go to Riverside Springs? Kathleen's sister Bridget had secured her a job with a lady named Bella, but that was before the fire. Leonie had such dreams of going. Maybe in Riverside Springs, she'd meet a man, they'd fall in love, and he would take care of her and her siblings. Her fingers inched across the scar on her forehead. She wasn't likely to meet a man now. Who'd want a cripple and a disfigured one at that? She closed her eyes, allowing the tears to fall for a few seconds. She heard the front doorbell ring and then the sounds of Maria's voice greeting Ethel, the new maid. Picking up a cloth, she wiped her face. She didn't want Maria to catch her sitting here, feeling sorry for herself. She pushed herself to her feet and tried to take a couple of steps. One, two, three, four. The palms of her hands stung gripping the crutches, but she continued. Five, six, seven, eight. Sweat dripped down her face, but she kept going. She was going to make it to ten before she admitted defeat. A knock on the door, and Maria entered just as Leonie took her tenth step.

"Leonie, you're walking."

"Shut the door before you tell the whole world," Leonie snapped. Seeing Maria's face, she modified her tone. "I want to keep it a secret until I can walk across the room."

Maria held out her arm. "Here, lean on me as you take the seat. We don't want you to fall."

As Leonie lowered herself awkwardly into the chair, she smiled at Maria. "You look lovely. That outfit really suits you."

Maria did a little twirl. "Do you really think so? With Frieda being away for a few days, I needed someone to give me an honest opinion. Conrad would tell me I look gorgeous wearing a sheet. I have a meeting with Anne Morgan and some of her friends. I wanted a look that was stylish yet hid my pregnancy. You know what those lot are like about being in public when you are pregnant." When Leonie looked at her blankly, Maria blushed. "In their world, you hide your pregnancy, and when it becomes obvious, you stay at home."

Leonie thought that was stupid. What was more natural than a married woman having a baby? "I think you look wonderful. Are you enjoying working with those ladies?"

Maria bit her lip, as she always did when considering an answer. "Yes. Well, sometimes. Anne is lovely, but some of her friends have opinions that are difficult to hear."

"Like how we are poor because we don't work hard enough? Or because we drink all our wages? Or have too many children?"

Maria nodded. "You've heard it before."

"Mama used to read the papers to me when she got ill and couldn't get out of bed. The boys would find papers in the rubbish and bring them home to her. It helped pass the time. Mama wasn't used to lying in bed; she always had to be busy."

Maria picked up the blouse Leonie had been working on. "You are a lot like your mother. These stitches are beautiful. Such delicate work. You have a gift, Leonie."

Leonie blushed at the praise.

"I showed some of my friends the present you gave me for my wedding. They'd pay for something similar for when they get married."

Leonie didn't meet Maria's gaze. "I worked on that before the fire. I don't think I could manage it now."

"Why not? Your hands and head work just fine. Are you still drawing? Remember, you told me your mother made you promise to become a dress designer one day."

Leonie stared at the carpet. "That was before."

"Lift up your head and look at me. We've had enough of that attitude. You can't let the fire ruin your future. It took so much from all of us already. We can't give it anymore."

Guilt turned Leonie's stomach into a hard lump. Maria had lost her sister in the fire, and they'd both lost several close friends and lots of acquaintances.

"Leonie, would you be interested in helping me with my work with Anne?"

"Me?"

"Your story, that of your survival, would help drum up support for our work. Some people have already forgotten about the fire. I know that's hard to believe, but they have. It's not even been a year. The families are still struggling; some are doing better than others. I think the newspapers would be interested in how you survived and are now recovering. They are looking for new angles, new stories, and you could be it."

Leonie shook her head. "I don't think people want to see the cripple with the horrible scar."

"I thought we had left the feeling sorry for yourself behind. You survived; you fought hard to get back to your family."

"Who are being sent to Riverside Springs without me."

Shocked, Maria could only stare at her.

"Carrie heard people talking about it. They suggested it would be better for the children to go ahead to Riverside Springs. I can follow when I get better."

Maria walked over to the bed before taking a seat. "That might be a good idea."

Leonie couldn't believe her ears.

"Don't look at me like that. Just think about it. The children are cooped up in this place. I know everyone treats them really well, but they aren't allowed out. They need to go to school and to mix with other children. River-side Springs sounds ideal. It's in the country-side with plenty of fresh air, it's far enough away for them to maybe forget or put aside their grief. Living here, seeing Kathleen and her husband, me, you – it must remind them of your mother and her dying in the hospital and then the fire..." Maria stood up again and walked over to where Leonie was sitting. "Nobody wants to separate you from the chil-dren, not permanently, but you can see why they might think it was a good idea."

"Is that why you really came here? To talk me into this plan to steal my family?"

Maria blinked rapidly, her eyes filled with hurt and temper. "I didn't know anything about this plan. It's not like I have nothing better to do than sit around discussing your life. I came here to see my friend. Obviously, it was a mistake." Maria was gone before Leonie got a chance to reply. She heard the front door slam. Maria's temper was legendary, and it seemed marriage hadn't softened her. Leonie pushed herself back up on the crutches and walked slowly back to her bed. No doubt someone would come to ask what had happened. What would she tell them? That she had accused one of her closest friends of betraying her? Shame filled her, making her stomach churn. She hated hurting people. Maria had done nothing but be a good friend. She picked up the blouse and threw it across the room, immediately regretting such a stupid reaction as she didn't have the energy to go over and pick it up.

## CHAPTER 2

*A* few days after the wedding, Kenny arrived at the sanctuary to say goodbye before heading to Riverside Springs. "I thought you might have a letter you wanted me to give to Mam or Shane?"

"That's kind of you, Kenny. I've hardly seen you the last few days," Kathleen said, noticing his flush.

"Sorry, I didn't mean you have neglected me. A young man like yourself would have people to see."

"I went back to the tenements to see the Flemings. Mr. Fleming was so good to us. I just wanted to check in with him and on Granny Belbin. I know she was always old, but she seems ancient now. She's grown smaller somehow. I send her letters when I am away, and she says it makes her feel like she's seen a bit of the world."

Kathleen's eyes welled up. "You are such a lovely lad. That was a very kind thing to do."

"Least I could do after all they did for me. Where's Lily?" He quickly changed the subject.

"She's just upstairs checking on the Chiver children. Leonie should be in her room if you want to say hello. Lily emptied one of the smaller storerooms and turned it into a bedroom for her. It makes it easier for her to move around with the chair."

Kenny walked over to the fire, warming his hands. "Richard told me he thought she would walk again."

"Yes, she can stand now for a few seconds. She's been doing exercises to strengthen the muscles in her legs. It will take time, but if she keeps up the hard work, I believe she will."

"Who will?" asked Lily as she entered the office. "Kenny, what a lovely surprise. I thought you had left already."

"The train leaves later this afternoon. I thought I'd check to see if you have any letters for Riverside Springs. I'm a bit quicker than the post."

"Will you stay for an early lunch? Cook always makes far too much food, and it will give me time to write a note to Bridget."

Kenny took a seat. The door opened once more, admitting Emily with Leonie following in her chair. "Sorry, I didn't know you were busy. We will come back later," Emily blushed as she turned to go.

"Stay. Emily, this is my nephew Kenneth, we call him Kenny." Kathleen looked at Kenny when he didn't respond, finding him staring at Leonie. She returned his stare as if there was nobody else in the room. Her face flushed as she seemed to realize what they had been doing and she looked away.

Kenny recovered quickly and walked toward Emily to shake her hand. "I've heard a lot about you and your work with children, Miss Emily." Kenny's voice shook slightly as he took Leonie's hand, holding it for longer than necessary. "I am very pleased to make your acquaintance, Miss Chiver. I have heard so much about your bravery. I hope your recovery continues."

Leonie blushed again, staring down at the hands in her lap. Lily broke the silence that had descended on the room. "I'll go and tell Cook we'd like an early lunch. It will just take a minute." She closed the door behind her.

Kathleen and Emily exchanged a conspiratorial glance. "Why don't you take a seat, Kenny. Emily and Leonie are here so we can talk about what we need to do while Lily is away. You know she is traveling to London with Patrick and Frieda and will then go on to Ireland with Charlie. Emily's husband oversees the new factory while us women are trying to organize the next orphan train to leave the city."

"Are the orphans going to Riverside Springs to Mam?" Kenny took a seat on the couch near the fire.

With a glance at Leonie, Kathleen nodded. She didn't know if Lily had spoken to the girl yet to see if she agreed with sending her siblings on ahead.

Emily picked up some papers from the desk. "There are the latest letters requesting children. You would think some were writing to Santa Claus looking for a present with the way their requests are phrased. 'A white boy with dark eyes and hair who looks just like my husband, preferably eighteen months old or less.' Another one says, 'a blonde girl with curly hair and a gentle disposition – will consider any child up to the age of four.'" Emily shook the letters. "Why can't they just open their hearts and homes to any child who needs one?"

Lily came into the room and took the letters from Emily. "I used to say the same thing, but I found some people are trying to replace a child they lost. They believe they can love a child more if it fits into their families. I suppose we shouldn't judge them; they don't have the luxury of getting to know the children like we do. They only meet them once the train pulls into the platform."

A look of shame passed over Emily's face. "I should not be so quick to judge."

Kathleen was quick to reassure the lovely young woman who had, until recently, spent all her time looking after orphaned girls. She had a kind heart. "Lily wasn't being critical, Emily, just explaining how we have come to terms with these letters. Have you been able to match up some of our children with the requests?"

Emily nodded. "Yes, most of them. I have also written to those who expressed interest in certain children to ask would they be willing to compromise on hair color or sex. Father Nelson's contacts have several children looking for homes. In total, we have about twenty more than the ones already matched with families. The train should leave the first week of April."

Lily looked up from her notes. "We need to find a suitable adult female to travel with the children. Sister Josephine broke her arm and a leg when she fell in the snow. She was out sledding with the children. I heard the Mother Superior is considering transferring our young Sister to a secluded order. She is far too boisterous and fun-loving to be a nun."

The women laughed, with Leonie explaining to Kenny, "Sister Josephine hasn't taken her full vows yet. I don't understand the whole process, but she is very young and not a bit like the nuns we see at Father Nelson's church. She is like a big child. Alfred, my brother, told us she climbed a tree to get their ball which was stuck."

Kenny smiled. "Sounds like she is perfect to work with children, but perhaps her time recovering may have her reconsider her choice."

Kathleen watched Leonie under her eyelashes. She hadn't seen the girl so animated in a long time. Leonie had always been shy, but since the fire, she had become even more reserved. She saw Kenny kept darting glances at the young girl when he thought nobody was looking.

Ethel interrupted, knocking on the door to announce lunch was ready. She carried in a large tray which Kenny gallantly relieved her of, setting it down on the coffee table. Ethel blushed, her hands shaking as she set the cups and saucers on the table with the plates.

"Thank you, Ethel, we can manage. Make sure Cook takes time to have a proper lunch. She is running herself ragged looking after all of us."

"Yes, Miss Lily. Thank you." Ethel curtsied again before she left the room.

"I wish she would stop doing that," Lily murmured as she poured the tea and coffees. "Kenny, tell us about your travels. It must be so different being at sea to living in a small town like Riverside Springs."

Amid the soft clinking of teacups on saucers, Kenny's deep voice kept them mesmerized with stories of his travels. The room seemed to hang on his every word, as he painted a picture of uncharted waters and bustling ports, his hands moving as if he could physically draw the maps he described. His presence was robust, a stark contrast to the delicate china in his large, calloused hands—a reminder of the physical nature of his service. The light from the overhead lamp glinted off the insignia on his uniform, casting a golden hue over his earnest, sun-kissed face. Laugh lines creased the corners of his eyes. His hair, cropped in military fashion, added to his authoritative air, but it was the twinkle in his sea-blue eyes that told of his love for the adventurous life at sea.

He made them laugh with the recollection of a bustling marketplace in Manila, the air rich with the aromas of street food and the sound of a language that danced as much as it spoke. He evoked sighs as he recounted the serene majesty of the Great Wall of China, stretching like a dragon's spine over the rugged terrain.

Kathleen, watching him from her vantage point, sensed the carefully curated nature of his stories. She knew the life of a sailor was not just the romance of new horizons and camaraderie but also filled with the monotony of endless waves, the sharp sting of homesickness, and the ever-present threat of danger that the ocean carried in her depths. Yet, as he spoke, the shadows of those unspoken hardships seemed to lift, and Kenny—the sailor, the adventurer, the storyteller—brought the world to their doorstep with the vibrancy and color of distant shores. Leonie was enthralled in his stories, leaning forward in her chair as if to listen better, her sandwiches uneaten on her plate, her coffee growing cold in its cup.

"I think I have monopolized the conversation for long enough. I love the Navy life so much, once I get started, I forget to stop talking," he shrugged, looking a little self-conscious.

"Your stories are wonderful, Kenny. Thank you for sharing them with us. If you give up Navy life, you could become a writer."

Kenny smiled his thanks at Emily's comment.

"How long will your stay be with us in Riverside Springs? Will there be time for another visit before you return to your naval duties?"

Shifting in his seat, Kenny's features settled into a contemplative expression, the morning light casting a golden hue on his clean-shaven jaw. "The future's a bit uncertain, Aunty," he admitted, his gaze drifting to the family photos on the mantelpiece, each frame a testament to the bonds in the room. "Dad seems to think I can convince Mom to rest more. I'm not sure that's possible, especially as I've got to be back to the ship by the 10th. We sail on the 11th for a six-month tour."

Leonie's reaction was quiet, a hand coming to rest over her lips, her eyes wide with the realization of the span of time. "Six months," she echoed, the words escaping her before she could catch them, tinged with an emotion she probably didn't intend to reveal. "I mean, it's quite a stretch—for your mother, of course."

# CHAPTER 3

*L*ily stood on the deck of the HMS Olympic, taking in the bustling activity as the ship prepared to depart. She huddled closer to her husband, sheltering against the chill of the salty sea air as she watched the stevedores on the dock below, wheeling trolleys packed with luggage up the gangplanks into the bowels of the ship.

Frieda clasped her hands together in front of her chest. "Are you scared, Lily? I can't work out if I'm terrified or excited, or maybe it's a mixture of both."

Lily shook her head, giving the younger woman a small smile. Charlie tightened his arm around her waist as if sensing her discomfort, even if he misunderstood the reason.

"They say Captain Smith is the best in the business. This ship is certainly one of the biggest and most luxurious, different from the one my family came to America on. It's completely safe. In four or five days, we will dock in Southampton, England."

Frieda scanned her surroundings. "Have you seen my husband?" She giggled like a little girl. "I still can't get used to calling Patrick that." Frieda wiped her eyes with a white hanky she had been using to wave to Kathleen, Richard, and the rest of their family and friends gathered at the Manhattan port saying goodbye.

Lily saw her tears but she couldn't bring herself to comfort her. What was wrong with her? Why didn't she feel anything? This was her first time traveling overseas, and she wasn't quite sure what to expect. But she had thought she'd feel something. Anything.

"There he is," Charlie answered, pointing out Patrick standing on the other side of the deck speaking to one of the ship's officers.

"That's the ship's doctor. Maybe he is offering his services."

As if he heard his name, they saw Patrick shake the officer's hand before making his way over to them, his face creased in a big smile but concern darkening his eyes as he saw Frieda's tears.

"Don't cry, darling. I know you're sad leaving everyone behind, but we can write. If things don't work out in England we will come home, I promise. Now, why don't we go down and see our cabin. It will be a while yet before the ship leaves."

Frieda took her husband's arm and together they walked over to the stairs. Their departure left Charlie and Lily alone on their side of the deck. The other passengers probably felt it was too cold to stand in the sea breeze. Lily pulled her scarf tighter, covering her ears before turning back to the view of the port.

"Are you having second thoughts about our trip?" Charlie's whisper was barely loud enough for her to hear.

"No, of course not," she lied, not looking at him.

"I thought it would be a good idea to get

away from New York, from the Sanctuary, the factory, the fire…"

Lily wanted to cover her ears with her hands. She didn't want to think about the last few months, never mind talk about them.

"Lily, can't you see how lucky we are? How many of those people down there would love to be us?" Charlie gazed at the people standing on the docks, staring back up at the ship.

Lily didn't respond.

"Lily, what's wrong?"

She shook her head. "I'm just tired."

"That's what you've been saying for weeks now. When you didn't come out of your room, I thought…it doesn't matter what I thought. But then Kathleen got you to the wedding and you seemed to be back to yourself. But now you… you have that look in your eyes again."

"What look?"

Charlie paused, both hands gripping the ship's rail, his knuckles white. "Like you are dead inside. The old Lily would have been jumping up and down with excitement." He tried to smile. "Well, maybe our days of jumping up and down are behind us. But you would have shown some emotion. I feel like I'm losing you, Lily."

The anguish in her husband's voice should have pierced her heart. She should feel something. This trip was something he'd talked about since those early days when she first met him, during the horrible blizzard. Carmel Doherty, his grandmother and the woman whom the sanctuary was officially named after, had filled his head with stories of the old country, of the Ireland of her youth and her love affair with her husband. Together the couple had survived the famine and come in search of a new life on one of the so-called coffin ships.

"I'm sorry. I don't know what is wrong with me. Everyone around me is so happy, but I just can't, I just don't..." She threw up her hands. "I know I'm lucky, Charlie. Look at me. I'm standing on this beautiful ship, ready to travel across the ocean to see different countries, to see Ireland." She moved closer. "I know how important this trip is to you, how you feel about seeing the places your Gran described." She tucked her arm into his. "You're stuck with me, Charlie Doherty. Don't go thinking otherwise."

He gave her a quick hug. They stood in silence, watching the quay before the blast of a horn made them both jump.

"We're moving. Say goodbye, darling. We're off." Charlie waved to the people on the quay-side like an excited child."

LILY AND CHARLIE met up with Frieda and Patrick on the deck, the early morning mist hanging over Southampton docks partially dimming their first glimpse of England. "This is it, our new home. Are you excited, darling?" Patrick held Frieda's hand. Glancing at Frieda's expression, Lily thought 'terrified' was a more apt description, but she heard the young girl say, "Yes. Very."

Lily turned her gaze back to the view of the dock. Frieda had confided her fears of every-thing changing. Newly married, starting her first job as a medical doctor in a strange country away from all her friends was a lot for anyone to cope with. Lily had reassured her as best she could. Frieda had survived worse, losing her family at a young age. She was as strong as they came. As the dock drew closer, the crew moved swiftly with practiced skill, preparing ropes and mooring lines. Seagulls flew above their heads as the gentle breeze carried the scent of salt and seaweed. The spires and rooftops of Southampton emerged from the mist, and she could spot figures on the docks, some waving to the ship while others busied themselves with their chores. She wondered how many people on board were returning home and how many, like them, were visiting England for the first time. For a moment, she panicked, wondering how such a large ship would manage pulling into the relatively small berth, but then she spotted the tugboats darting around the ship, their whistles communicating with each other. The creaking of ropes and shouts from the crew signaled their safe arrival. With a final jolt, the HMS Olympic came to rest, to the cheers of both the waiting crowd and the passengers.

They wouldn't be staying in Southampton but catching a train up to London. Charlie had arranged for their luggage to be transported to the train station so they just had to look after themselves. They didn't have to wait long as a line of cabs stood waiting near the docks. Charlie hailed one to take the four of them to the station.

"Watch out, Frieda," Patrick pulled his wife out of the way.

Frieda put a hand to her mouth, her face pale from shock. "I forgot they drive on the wrong side of the road."

The cab driver rolled his eyes but didn't make any comment. Lily stared out the window, taking in the sights as they drove to the station. It reminded her of the hustle and bustle of the New York docks, with men heaving large trunks, children darting around their feet selling newspapers or stealing when they thought the new arrivals were distracted.

"Poor children, they look much the same as they do in New York," Lily muttered, only realizing she had spoken aloud when Charlie took her hand and whispered, "You are on vacation now, darling. Try to enjoy it."

# CHAPTER 4

Kathleen stared in despair at her diary. Was it only a week since she'd waved goodbye to Patrick, Frieda, Lily, and Charlie, watching the RMS Olympic until it had disappeared from view? It seemed longer. She missed her son and her friends.

But that wasn't the only thing contributing to her bad mood. The accounts for the sanctuary were impossible to balance. They had gone over budget on the new factory, partly because they wanted to ensure it met all the fire prevention strategies the local fire chief had recommended. Sprinkler systems, more fire exits, regular waste collection, and even extra fire buckets and hoses all added up. They had also lost the monthly donations both Frieda and Patrick had contributed.

They needed to increase fundraising, but with most of their friends helping the victims of the shirtwaist fire and other causes, contributions were less than they had been at this time last year. She rubbed her temple, trying to massage away the developing headache. Things were challenging, and then she had opened the most recent letter from Bridget. In addition to asking about the Chiver family and when she should expect them to arrive, Bridget was worried about finances. It was unusual for her sister to be so frank.

*"I'm sorry, Kathleen, to add to your burdens. We have had several new children brought to the orphanage. Some are orphans; others have run away from families who exploited them. We have two so-called breaker boys, who lost fingers mining coal but whose families relied on their wages. Now they cannot work, the families have thrown them out. I don't know what to do. Everyone has tightened their belts until there is no belt left."*

This bit of the letter was smudged as if Bridget had been crying. Kathleen blew her nose; she had read all about the children working in mining and the dangers they were exposed to. It was against the law to employ them, but since when did the law stand in the way of people making money.

She pushed the papers aside and stood up. A walk would blow off the cobwebs and give her mind time to think about answers to their many problems.

"Let me go, I didn't do anything. Ouch, that hurt."

Kathleen heard the child's shouts of protest amidst the hubbub of conversation and the blaring of police whistles on the busy street. A butcher, his dirty apron streaked with blood, stood outside his store with beefy arms folded across his chest, staring at the unfolding scene. Two policemen were trying to subdue a ragged-looking boy with a torn coat, trousers too short, and bare feet. The child kicked and bit, trying to get free, while another younger boy, his clothes equally shabby but at least he wore shoes, stood screaming, tears falling down his cheeks. Kathleen inhaled sharply as one officer gave the elder child a vicious cuff across the head. She couldn't stand by and do nothing. Lifting her skirt, she ran over to the store.

"Stop that! Stop it at once! He's only a child."

One policeman turned at her shouting, his eyes widening at her appearance. "He's a thief, a no-good rotten little tyke. Stay out of this, madam. This is police business."

"Let him go this instant." Kathleen tried to catch her breath and stand taller. She was too old for running in the streets. Glancing around, she noticed her actions had attracted a small crowd, eyeing her clothes, possibly wondering why a woman dressed as well as her was racing down the street, screaming like a banshee. She placed a hand over her beating heart and, using her poshest voice, addressed the officer. "I don't care what he did, you have no right to treat a child so callously."

The officer spat to the side, barely missing Kathleen's feet. "Get lost, lady. This is none of your concern." He turned his back to her, speaking to another cop who had just arrived. "Grab that brat too. He's probably hiding the stuff."

The elder boy kicked out again. "I told ya. I

didn't steal nothing. I asked the store owner for work, I washed his windows and instead of paying me like he promised, he laughed at us."

Kathleen heard the honesty in the boy's voice, but it made no difference to the man restraining him. If anything, it earned the child another belt. This time the cop's hand caught the boy across the cheekbone. The child whimpered despite himself, his eyes welling up.

Kathleen had seen enough. All her years living with Richard melted away, and she turned into the tenement child she once was, her temper raging, ready to fight the world for this child. Without thinking, she whacked the officer with her bag, punctuating each word with another blow. "That... is... enough! Let him go, you great big bully!"

Surprised, the officer released the child, who could have escaped if he hadn't tried to grab the younger child. Kathleen didn't have time to think about that as the officer's partner arrested her, handcuffing her and then bundling her into the wagon that had arrived on the scene. The children were separated and thrown in after her, the younger landing on the floor in a heap. The elder child hit his head on the side of the wagon and slumped to the floor. Kathleen tried to help but was thwarted by her handcuffs.

"The child is ill, help him!" She implored the officer sitting in the wagon with them, but he just smoked his cigarette, blowing smoke in her face. She pulled at her hands, but the cuffs held tight. The boy groaned as the younger child scuttled across the floor to his side.

# CHAPTER 5

*I*t didn't take long to arrive at the station. She was pulled out of the wagon and pushed roughly up the steps into the redbrick station. Inside, the walls were lined with dark, rough-looking wood paneling, and the floors were a checkered pattern of black and white tiles, scuffed up from the feet of policemen and prisoners alike.

A large wooden desk, covered in stacks of paperwork, sat near the entrance, right behind an iron grill that separated the officers from the public. Gas lamps hanging from the ceiling cast a soft, flickering glow throughout the room, but the atmosphere was anything but cozy. Kathleen shivered despite herself.

A tall policeman, with a grizzled mustache, tired blue eyes, and lines marking years of service on his face, looked up as Kathleen was pushed forward. She almost lost her balance but managed to remain standing. As he took a drag from his cigarette, his sharp eyes assessed Kathleen, no doubt taking in her ruffled hair and disheveled appearance.

"Name?"

"Kathleen Green. My husband is Dr. Richard Green. Please summon Inspector Griffin immediately; I must speak to him."

She saw the light of recognition in his gaze and relaxed. This man knew the Inspector. Everything would be fine. The police officer took another drag on his cigarette, staring at her insolently as the seconds ticked past. He flicked the ash from his cigarette before addressing the officer escorting her.

"Charge?"

"Aiding and abetting a criminal, as well as assaulting a police officer."

"Assault?" The man stubbed out his cigarette. "That's a serious charge. Take her downstairs."

Kathleen shrugged free of the officer's hand on her shoulder. "I didn't assault anyone."

The man's blue eyes bored into hers. She stammered, "I mean, I did hit a policeman but only because he was mistreating a child. I asked him to stop but he ignored me."

She realised her mistake as the man's eyes gleamed.

"You admit to assaulting a police officer?" He wrote something on the docket in front of him. "Take her away. Next."

Kathleen huddled in the corner of the dimly lit prison cell, her teeth chattering uncontrollably in the biting cold February afternoon. The dampness of the cell seeped into her bones, sending shivers down her spine. She refused to acknowledge the other adults sharing their cell, ignoring their whistles, catcalls, and dirty-minded comments.

"Don't let them see your fear, missus," the boy she'd rescued – now sporting a black eye and holding his head in his hands – whispered, his breath visible in the frosty air. The younger child, a girl despite her jacket and pants, sat on Kathleen's knee, her thumb in her mouth, the other hand clutching a worn-out rag doll.

Kathleen forced herself to sit up straighter, but the frigid air made it hard to move. She couldn't believe she was in this godforsaken cell. What was Richard going to say? Would the charge of assaulting a police officer stick? You could go to jail for that. She shouldn't have hit him; she knew that. Her Irish temper had surfaced despite her being a middle-aged woman – almost thirty-six years old. She leaned back against the cold, stone wall as memories of her early years flooded through her. After her mam had died, Bridget and herself had tried to keep their family together, but that hadn't been possible. They'd been too poor, too vulnerable. Bridget had to run away from New York to save them from a fate worse than death, and their only crime was becoming orphans. Despite that being almost twenty years ago, and all of the efforts at the Sanctuary, it appeared nothing had changed.

She beckoned the boy to move closer. "What's your name? Where are your parents?"

"Max."

"Nice to meet you, Max. Won't your parents be worried?"

"Ain't got none. Mama worked at the shirt-

47

waist factory. It got burnt down. She didn't come home."

Horrified, Kathleen knew she was staring. The fire had been the previous April. No wonder the children were so scrawny. Who had been looking after them? How had they survived so long?

A defiant look came over the boy as he kicked the ground of the cell. "We do fine. Today was a misunderstanding, that's all."

"That fire was ten months ago. You can't be more than seven years old. Do you have other family?"

"I'm almost nine. Old enough."

His cheeks flushed at the lie, but she didn't call him on it. She shifted slightly so the child on her lap was sitting a little more comfortably and not pressing on her bladder. "But this little one…"

"Nettie, she's five." Five? That could be correct, even though the child looked to be a lot younger.

She asked again about his family. "Is it just the two of you?"

"No. Mama's sister looks after us."

Nettie shook her head. "Ginny went away. She said she wouldn't. She lied."

"Shut up, Nettie." The girl whimpered at her brother's tone, turning her face into Kathleen's chest, shoving her thumb into her mouth. Kathleen rubbed the child's hair, trying to comfort her while not shuddering as she saw lice crawling across her scalp. The girl was skin and bone, her elbows digging into Kathleen's ribs.

"So you've been living alone. When did she leave?"

He didn't answer.

"When?" Kathleen held his gaze; he was the first to look away.

"She said she was going to get some oranges. For Nettie for Christmas. She went out. She didn't come back."

Kathleen's heart broke a bit more. The boy was trying to be brave, but he wasn't that good an actor. She caught the tremor in his voice. He wouldn't meet her eyes either, looking everywhere but at her face. "Where do you live?"

"At home," he said at the same time as Nettie said, "No home."

"What she means is we had to move a

couple of times, but we'll find something better as soon as we get out of here. You shouldn't have interfered; you made things worse."

"Worse?" The cheek of him. "You got beaten up by the cop while being arrested. If I hadn't intervened, who knows how bad your injuries would have been."

"I'm stronger than I look. Now, we are facing a judge. They could put us in jail. They don't like it when you hit one of their own."

She knew that; she wasn't a child. But they wouldn't put the children in jail, or at least not Nettie. It depended on what they thought her brother had done. They'd most likely be sent to the New York asylum, especially when the court found out there were no parents. At the asylum, the children would be separated and could be put on orphan trains.

Unless she could help and take them to the Sanctuary, Father Nelson might know of a home for them. Even as she thought that, reality crept in. Father Nelson's resources were stretched to the breaking point. How could she help anyone if she landed in jail? That wouldn't happen. She didn't have a record, so the judge would likely make her pay a fine, wouldn't he?

The minutes on the clock ticked by, and nobody came. No Inspector Griffin, no Richard. Surely someone had told her husband where she was. Cook would have missed her, wouldn't she? Or Leonie. They'd be expecting her back at the Sanctuary. Or maybe they thought she had gone home.

"Was it true what you said about the man? Did he promise to pay you?" Kathleen asked.

"I ain't no liar and I don't take no charity. I did the work he wanted, and he wouldn't pay me. He threw me out of his store, and then the cops came. There was only one at first; I could have gotten away, but he blew his whistle, and then two more of them came. I still had a chance until you showed up." He glared at her.

Despite herself, Kathleen laughed. He reminded her of her brothers, Michael and Shane. They would have played the tough guys too. She stopped smiling. Look what had nearly happened to them. Only for Richard, her brothers could have been hanged for a murder they didn't commit. She couldn't let Max and Nettie back onto the streets. She had to take care of them.

The night passed with several more women

being admitted. These latest arrivals were a mixture of drunks and those who worked the streets, their pitiful rags barely covering them. Max had moved closer to her when a fight broke out between two of the women. Despite the rest of the inmates clamoring for the guards, nobody came. Kathleen held Nettie on her knee, with Max pulled into her side. She glared at anyone who looked twice at them, ready to do battle on their behalf. No more harm would come to these children.

Morning arrived with the screeching of cell doors being opened. Food, or what sufficed for food, was thrown into the cell along with instructions to get ready to go to court. Kathleen ignored the moldy bread and evil-smelling mush.

"Soon, we will be home, and you can have plenty to eat."

Nettie gripped Kathleen's arm. "You promise you won't leave us here."

"Not a chance. You are coming with me. My husband is a doctor; I want him to look at Max's arm. I think it might be broken. His head also needs to be checked."

"But what about me?" Nettie's wide-eyed

stare reminded Kathleen of her daughter, Esme. How would her beloved child have fended had Richard and herself not been able to adopt her? She cuddled Nettie closer. "You need to be checked by a doctor too."

The child looked at her brother. Max gave a small nod.

"We'll go with you, but once we are outside this place, we will go our own way. Mam said that if we let anyone take us, they wouldn't let us stay together. She said there were homes for boys and girls. She used to tell me I'd end up there if I played up or didn't do my chores." Max bit his lip. Kathleen wanted to reassure him, to tell him that all mothers threatened their children with consequences if they misbehaved. Hadn't she told little Richie only last week that she'd give back all his Christmas presents if he kept bouncing on his bed? She swallowed a sob. She'd never threaten her children again.

A young officer, who seemed barely old enough to shave, opened the cell door, barking out names of other inmates.

She stood up, running a hand through her hair to tame her unruly curls. Not that it mattered. She needed a hot bath and fresh clothes to look anyway decent. She lifted Nettie up and held Max's hand with the other. Head held high, she ignored their cellmates and walked over to the door.

"Only you. The tykes stay here."

"You didn't call my name. I wanted to ask you a favor. Please."

"Listen, lady."

Kathleen pretended not to have heard him. "My name is Kathleen Green. My husband is the renowned burns doctor, and our close friend is Inspector Griffin. Perhaps you would like me to tell Pascal how you treated me with kindness and concern, officer?" She held his gaze as he stared at her. He wetted his lips; he was nervous. Probably new to this job and not yet jaded by the daily misery he saw.

"Officer, all this has been a serious misunderstanding. Find Inspector Griffin, and he will give me a character witness." Kathleen glanced at the children and saw the officer's expression soften as he looked at Nettie. "They are all alone; their mother died in the Shirtwaist fire. Please help us."

He glanced around and, seeing no one else

was paying them any attention, nodded and gestured for her to return to the cell. "I'll be back as soon as I can."

Kathleen reached out but didn't quite touch him. "Thank you." She returned to her spot by the wall and, gathering the children to her, sat down once more, saying a prayer it wouldn't take long to find Pascal Griffin.

## CHAPTER 6

$\mathcal{T}$ime seemed to stand still in the prison cell, despite her efforts to distract the children. Nettie was tired, cold and hungry. Kathleen told her stories about the Chiver children and how Carrie would teach Nettie some games to play. "She gives her dolls tea parties. You'd like that wouldn't you?"

Nettie shrugged, her thumb stuck in her mouth. Max's eyes were closed, the pallor of his face giving her cause for concern. She wondered if he had a concussion, quite likely given the blow his head had taken. He held his arm awkwardly. She suspected it was fractured. How was the child not screaming in agony, but she hadn't seen him shed a single tear. She glanced at her watch again, but the hand hadn't moved since the last time. What was taking so long?

"KATHLEEN GREEN. WHERE ARE YOU?" Startling Nettie who dozed in her arms, Kathleen scrambled to her feet at the sound of her friend's voice. "Here. I'm in here. Thank God they found you."

"Found me? We've been searching the streets of New York looking everywhere for you. Richard is beside himself, the poor man hasn't even stopped to eat. What did you do?" This last question was fired at the young officer. "Henderson, do you not know who this woman is? Have you heard of Carmel's Mission? The sanctuary for women and children. This woman and her friends are responsible for saving several children from a fate worse than death and you have her locked up?"

"Sorry sir. I mean it wasn't me sir. She was arrested and the desk sergeant said she had to stay in here." The poor officer mumbled as his cheeks flushed, his eyes frantically moving between Kathleen and his superior officer.

"Pas… I mean Inspector, he helped me which is more than can be said for your sergeant. I asked him to contact you yesterday at lunchtime when I was first arrested. But he ignored me."

"I will have his head. What is the world coming to? Locking up an innocent wo…"

Kathleen couldn't hold his gaze, dropping hers to the floor. When she glanced up again, he was staring at her.

"Maybe I could explain at home?"

Pascal's gaze now locked on the two children at her side.

"That boy's arm looks broken and what happened to his head?"

"Your men did this. I think we need to find Richard and get him medical help. He should have been seen hours ago."

"Henderson, pick up this boy and follow us to my carriage. Kathleen, give me the lad." He held out his arms. Kathleen kissed Nettie's sleeping cheek. "Her name is Nettie. Max is her big brother, and only remaining family."

"Good Lord. Let's get out of here before I throttle someone. Follow me."

Kathleen didn't need telling twice.

Inspector Griffin marched out of the cell door, up the stairs and past the desk sergeant. It was the same mustached man as the day before. Kathleen glared at him as she followed Officer Henderson who carried Max outside to the waiting carriage.

"Henderson you put the boy here by my side. Then help Mrs. Green. We are going to the hospital. Find Dr Richard Green and tell him to meet us there."

"Yes sir."

KATHLEEN EXPLAINED what had happened as they drove to the hospital. When she outlined how the police officers had hit Max, Pascal Griffin's mouth thinned.

"Where was this?"

"Outside the butchers, Mitchell & Sons. You know it?"

Inspector Griffin nodded, an expression of distaste in his eyes. "I wouldn't eat anything I bought in that place." The inspector eyed the boy, fast asleep his head on Kathleen's shoulder. "You say the boy said he was promised payment for work."

"Yes and I believe him. I know he's small but we've both seen younger boys working. He sounded so earnest, so sincere." At the look the inspector gave her, she bristled slightly. "I know there are some who could charm honey from the bees, but this boy is different. He could have got away for one thing but he stayed behind for his sister.

"Sister?"

"Nettie, she's a girl but they dressed her as a boy, perhaps for protection or maybe that is all the clothes they had. Their mother died in the Triangle fire. No mention of the father. There was an aunt but seems she left at Christmas and they have been fending for themselves since." Kathleen took a breath. "I know I was wrong to hit the policeman but I just…my temper got the better of me. Everything has felt so unfair lately. The court case, the rumors about the insurance payouts the Shirtwaist kings received, Lily going away…". Kathleen couldn't continue as the tears fell.

Inspector Griffin shifted in his seat clearly uncomfortable. She knew he would have rescued the children too, but he had to uphold the law and she had placed him in a compromising position. She hadn't even thought about that when she insisted, he was called.

"I'm sorry, Pascal. I should have handled it differently."

"I can't argue with that." He glanced out the window of the cab. "We're here. I'll get out first and get someone to help with the children."

The carriage stopped, Inspector Griffin got out and was soon back with a doctor and two male attendants. "Gently now, the elder child has a head injury and what appears to be a broken arm."

Max woke as the orderly picked him up. "No. I have to stay with Nettie, she needs me." The boy twisted, kicking and biting.

"Max stop. I have Nettie and I won't let her out of my sight. You go with these men, they are here to help us. I promise nothing bad will happen."

Max held her gaze, his eyes cloudy with indecision.

"It will be fine. Trust me."

Max nodded and let himself be carried into the hospital. Kathleen handed Nettie to another orderly before she climbed down from the seat. Then taking Nettie in her arms once more, she walked up the steps and into the hospital.

"MRS. GREEN....THIS IS A SURPRISE." Matron greeted her, her eyes wide. Kathleen desperately wanted to itch her scalp but ignored the urge. It was bad enough she looked like she felt, dirty, disheveled, and not in the least like the wife of a doctor with her husband's reputation.

"Matron, thank goodness you are here. I need your skills with this poor unfortunate child. She is starving, pure skin and bone. She could do with a bath and some new clothes. Her brother is with the doctors, he has a head trauma."

Matron's mouth thinned as she glanced at Nettie. Then she turned and called to a young girl carrying a bucket walking towards them. "Cooper, help Mrs. Green. This child is infested. You'll need plenty of hot water, a scissors to get rid of the hair and a comb."

The young girl gaped at them, opening and closing her mouth like a fish. Matron clapped her hands. "Go on. We haven't got all day." Matron addressed Kathleen, "Perhaps you would like to go home Mrs. Green to change and return later. Cooper can look after the child."

Nettie's nails clawed Kathleen's skin. Kathleen used her free hand to push the hair back from the child's eyes. "I'll stay with you. I promised Max. Nurse Cooper, perhaps you could lead the way. Thank you, Matron, for your assistance."

Kathleen could feel the Matron's eyes boring into her back. No doubt word would spread like wildfire though the hospital. Kathleen stood straighter. If she cared about gossip, she wouldn't work in the job she did.

"Poor little tyke, she looks like she been through the wars. Did you find her on the street?"

"Yes." Kathleen wasn't going to fuel gossip by admitting they had spent the night in a police cell. Nurse Cooper didn't seem to notice, she chatted away as she led them through a series of corridors until they came to a room with a large bath. Nettie stiffened at the sight of it.

Nurse Cooper turned on the tap, checking the temperature of the water. "I'll just go grab some towels and other things. Do you want to undress her, or should I do it?"

Nettie bit her lip. Kathleen placed her on the ground beside the tub. "You will enjoy this, Nettie. The water will be lovely and warm. When you are all clean, we will find you something to eat. You'd like that wouldn't you?"

Nettie nodded but her eyes roved the room, avoiding the bath. Kathleen gently undressed her, trying not to shudder at the insect bite marks on the child's skin. Swiping a hand across her eyes to clear the tears, Kathleen picked Nettie up and placed her into the tub. The child took a couple of seconds to relax and then she smiled.

"The water feels good doesn't it darling?" Kathleen crooned. Wishing for some of her own lavender soap, she took the carbolic and used it to scrub the dirt from the girl's body. There were no signs of abuse, no bruising or scarring aside from old bites. Nettie's ribs were clearly visible highlighting the length of time since her last proper meal. Nurse Cooper had yet to return. Kathleen turned the hair washing into a game, making Nettie shriek with laughter as she dunked her head and splashed about in the tub.

A knock on the door announced Nurse Cooper who walked in beaming, holding a glass of milk and a small plate of food in one hand, towels and other things in her other. "It's lovely to hear her laughing. I thought she might be hungry, poor little thing." She placed the food on the stool near the bath. "Go on, eat. Nobody will see you."

Kathleen smiled her thanks as Nettie shoved a piece of bread in her mouth, followed by a long drink of milk.

"What do you say to Nurse Cooper, Nettie?"

"Thank you." Nettie whispered, going shy.

Nurse Cooper took some scissors from her pocket. "I won't scalp her but it would be best to cut off most of her hair. It's so matted, it will hurt to get it untangled and you can clearly see it's infested." Still, she hesitated as if waiting for permission. Tiredness overwhelmed Kathleen as she nodded in agreement. She sat back as Nurse Cooper took over, singing and playing with Nettie as if she had known her all her life. The nurse was born to work with children.

She was skilled with the scissors too. Some would just hack off the hair in lumps, but Nurse Cooper took the time to style the shorter hairstyle. As she worked, she chatted with Nettie never once giving the child the impression she was someone to look down on. Kathleen couldn't help but compare this kind hearted young woman to Matron.

Once dressed in the too long nightgown, Nettie looked adorable. Her short haircut made her amber colored eyes look even bigger. When Kathleen showed her, her reflection in the mirror, Nettie reached out to touch it. "Is that me?"

Kathleen leaned in and kissed her cheek. "It certainly is. Thank you, Nurse Cooper."

The girl twiddled her fingers, not quite meeting Kathleen's gaze. "Would you like a bath as well Mrs. Green? I could find you a nightgown or bring you a sponge for your dress or...." Clearly embarrassed the girl didn't know where to look.

Kathleen wanted nothing more than to wash her hair and body. But she had to find out what was happening with Max and then find Richard. Her heart thudded at the thought of what her poor husband would say. He must be going frantic worrying about her.

"Thank you, but I will wait until I get home. We need to check on Nettie's brother. But I will borrow the comb if I may?"

"Would you like me to do it for you?"

Kathleen blushed but nodded. They both knew the girl would be best able to remove any lice hiding in Kathleen's long hair.

"Thank you for your kindness, Nurse Cooper. You have a real gift for dealing with children. You will go far in your chosen job."

"You're kind Mrs. Green but I'm not a nurse. I'm only an orphan, I live in the asylum, and work here at the hospital. All I'm fit for is to be a scrubber, ain't nobody going to let the likes of me be a nurse."

Kathleen pushed down her horror at the mention of the New York Children's asylum. "Is that what you would like to do?"

Miss Cooper shook her head. "I'd like to work with children but not when they are sick. I mean I love looking after them but it's hard to see a child in pain."

Kathleen couldn't agree with her more, yet her answer had surprised her. To have such a soft heart after growing up in the asylum. You had to be tough to survive in that place.

"Have you worked here long?" Kathleen asked before wincing as the girl pulled the comb through a particularly bad knot in her hair. Not for the first time, Kathleen wished she was brave enough to cut her hair short.

"About seven years. I started in the kitchen's when I was twelve. I prefer the work I do now. I don't want to ever have to peel another potato or wash a cabbage again." The girl grinned as she made jokes about her job. Kathleen found it difficult to keep her thoughts to herself. A kind, naturally intelligent young girl like Cooper should have a much brighter future to look forward to. It wasn't her fault she was an orphan.

Kathleen had an idea how she could help the kind girl but now wasn't the time to pursue it.

"Thank you for helping me with my hair. I must go find Max but how do I get in touch with you, Miss Cooper?"

"You'll find me here. Matron will tell you where I am if you ever need me. Good luck little one." Cooper reached out to pat Nettie's hand before turning her attention to washing down the bath.

THEY FOUND Max sitting up in bed, a bandage wrapped around his head and his right arm in a sling. Inspector Griffin sat by his bedside with Richard on the other.

"Kathleen, thank God. Why didn't you ask the police to send for me?"

Kathleen really hated the mustached police officer now. "I did darling. I asked for both you and Inspector Griffin but they threw me into the cells. They were rather annoyed."

Patrick reached over and gave her an awkward hug before greeting Nettie.

"Good evening young lady."

Nettie sucked her thumb and turned her face away.

Max had also been given a wash and was wearing night attire too. He looked downcast and so young until he spotted Nettie. His eyes widened as his gaze traveled from the top of his little sister's head to her toes and back. "You look so clean."

Nettie scrambled to climb up on the covers.

"Get down from there at once." A nurse walked over, her starched uniform making a crisp rustling sound with each purposeful step. She was a stern figure, her eyes softening only when they landed on the young patient. "It's quite unseemly to climb on the patient's bed."

Nettie retreated immediately, her small body seeming to shrink with the scolding. She hid behind Kathleen. "I only wanted to be closer to Max," she said, her voice a mere whisper, thick with the beginnings of tears.

Max, despite his injuries, mustered a gentle smile for his sister. "It's alright, Nettie. I can see you just fine from here."

Inspector Griffin observed the exchange, his seasoned gaze softening as he met Kathleen's gaze. Richard took the nurse aside and assured her the youngster couldn't hurt her patient.

GRIFFIN CLEARED HIS THROAT, drawing Nettie's attention. "Now, Miss Nettie, I need to ask you some questions. Your brother told me what happened yesterday at the store. I need you to do the same. Do you think you could sit on Mrs. Green's lap and talk to me?"

Nettie nodded. Richard carried over a chair for Kathleen who took a seat and then lifted Nettie onto her lap. Richard stood behind her, his hand on her shoulder. She leaned into his strength loving the fact that he supported her despite her appearance and her arrest.

Nettie leaned back against Kathleen's chest, before sticking her thumb in her mouth once more.

"Now," Inspector Griffin began, his voice dropping to a conspiratorial whisper. "Tell me everything you remember about what happened yesterday from when you and your brother arrived at the store. Mind you tell the truth now."

"ME AND MAX WERE STARVING. We're always hungry but Max had no money so he said he was going to get some work. I was supposed to stay home but I don't like being there on my own. So I followed him." Nettie flushed glancing at her brother but he gave her an encouraging smile. Inspector Griffin listened

71

intently, his eyes never leaving Nettie's face. Every so often, he'd nod, encouraging the child to continue, jotting down notes in a small leather-bound notebook.

"THE BIG MAN, he cuts up meat, he said Max could sweep the floor and scrub the pavement and then he would give us a penny. I didn't like the smell, it was rotten. When Max was finished, the man just laughed and then he told us to go away." Nettie hesitated, glancing at Max but he had fallen asleep.

"Go on." Inspector Griffin glanced up from his notebook.

"I don't want to get Max in trouble." Nettie's voice was barely more than a whisper.

"Just tell the truth, darling." Kathleen gave the girl a quick kiss on the top of her head.

"Max said he wasn't leaving until the man paid us. That made the big man angry. He started shouting and he grabbed his brush, I thought he was going to hit Max. I screamed and then we heard whistles and the policemen arrived. They grabbed Max's arm and the man said Max was a thief. But he isn't. He never takes nothing even when I tell him my belly hurts."

Kathleen held the child tighter.

"The police were hurting Max and then this lady came and she was hitting the policeman with her bag. Like this." Nettie straightened up and mimed Kathleen hitting the policeman. Inspector Griffin put a hand over his mouth, Kathleen hoped he was trying to hide a smile. Richard coughed as if he too was trying not to laugh.

"That made them mad. They pushed us into a wagon. Max wasn't moving fast enough. They made him fall and he hit his head. They didn't care. They just laughed. Then they took us to their house and it was horrible. There was a man behind a big screen, he was a nasty man. He had a furry thing on his mouth. Mrs. Kathleen spoke nice but he didn't listen. He said she had done something bad. But she didn't, not really."

Nettie looked at Inspector Griffin but his eyes stayed on his notebook. Kathleen smiled at her but stayed silent. The child wasn't finished with her story.

"We had to go downstairs to a big room

with bars on it. It was locked and there were other people in the room we were in, and they kept laughing and pointing at us. One came over, she didn't smell very good but Mrs. Kathleen she told her to go away. She put on a real scary face and the woman moved." Nettie looked up at Kathleen. "I know you were only pretending as you aren't a bit mean, but she thought you were."

"Mrs. Kathleen has her moments, young Nettie." At Inspector's Griffins words, Nettie sat forward, her voice raised in protest.

"Mrs. Kathleen, she asked the policemen to get her husband and to find you but they weren't nice. Mama would have told them to mind their manners."

Inspector Griffin coughed as he put his notebook away. "Sounds to me like your mama raised you right, Nettie. Thank you for telling me your story."

Nettie's eyes filled up. "Have I got Max in trouble? Are you going to send him away?"

"You haven't done anything wrong, Nettie. Telling the truth is always the right thing to do. Max will have to stay in the hospital for a few days. Just until the doctors tell us he is getting better."

Nettie stared at her brother, her face screwed up with concern, her eyes filled with fear. "Can I stay with him?" she whispered.

Kathleen squeezed her hand. "No darling, but you can come home with me. We have a daughter and son who would love to say hello to you. We will come back tomorrow to check on Max."

"You promise?" Nettie stared at Kathleen, trust vying with a hint of suspicion.

Kathleen nodded as Inspector Griffin stood up.

"What about the charge against me?" Kathleen asked in a low voice not wanting the nurses to overhear her.

"I think I can make that go away. I will let you know in a few days." Inspector Griffin shook Richard's hand and with a pat on Nettie's head, he walked out of the ward.

Richard took charge.

"Nettie give Max a kiss goodnight and then we will all go home. My wife needs a bath and I'm hungry."

"Me too." Nettie answered.

. . .

KATHLEEN'S CHILDREN greeted her with hugs and kisses when she walked into her home. Richard carried Nettie inside as she'd fallen asleep in the cab. Esme's mouth fell open when she spotted the child. She ran over. "Did you get me a sister?"

Nettie woke up at Esme's shout, shrinking back into Richard's arms, her thumb in her mouth. Kathleen motioned to Richard to put Nettie down as he answered Esme.

"No darling. This is a friend of your mother's. She is going to stay with us for a few days."

Nettie clung to Kathleen's skirt. Esme came closer, curiosity written all over her face. Richie rolled his eyes. "Why couldn't you bring home a boy? Girls are no fun. Can I be excused?"

"Yes son." Richard and Kathleen exchanged a glance of amusement as Richie dashed off, probably to play ball once more.

"What's her name and why is her hair so short?"

"Esme don't be rude. This is Nettie. Her brother Max is in hospital, he's a patient of your father's. Nettie is very scared and tired and she needs you to be kind to her." Kathleen eyed her daughter, who looked like butter wouldn't melt in her mouth but could be precocious when she wanted to be.

"Can she sleep in my bedroom? I can show her my dolls and we can have a tea party and…"

Kathleen bent down and gave Esme a hug. "You can do all those things. But try using your quiet voice. Nettie hasn't had much sleep and is very tired. She is hungry too. Why don't you take Nettie to meet Cook and see if she has any cookies for you. I want to have a bath and change before dinner."

Esme smiled, holding out her hand to Nettie. "Come on. I'll look after you. I'm almost eight. What type of cookies do you like? Chocolate are my favorite."

Nettie glanced at Kathleen for permission. She nodded and watched the children walk out of the door towards the kitchen.

Richard came up behind her, hugging her close.

"Don't darling. I'm probably crawling with bugs. I best have a bath."

"I can wash your hair for you." He winked at her making her giggle like a schoolgirl rather than a matronly married woman. She was such a lucky woman. How many other husbands would treat their wives so kindly in a similar situation?

"I can manage but come and talk to me if you like."

SHE EXPLAINED what had happened and how they had ended up in the jail cell overnight. His expression darkened when she outlined her requests for help, that the police find him or Inspector Griffin but he didn't interrupt. She told him the whole story right up until they met at the hospital.

"I didn't know what to think when you didn't come home. Ethel, Leonie, Cook and Emily were frantic too. They said you went for a walk at lunchtime and when you didn't return they assumed you had gone home. Emily was worried as you missed a meeting you had scheduled but she thought you were tired. When you didn't turn up last night, I didn't know what to think. I checked all the hospitals and we checked with the police." Richard stood and paced back and forth. "If I had that sergeant in front of me. I'd... well I wouldn't be held accountable. He must have known you were the woman we were looking for. You don't look like the usual type to spend a night in the cells."

"I'm sorry, Richard. I should have handled things better."

"You did what you always do, put children first. I knew that from the first moment I met you on the train. You were spitting fire at that woman who mistreated Patrick. I fell in love with you that day and I haven't stopped loving you since. When I thought I might have lost you... I swear Kathleen I couldn't bear it."

She put out her hand and he came over and hugged her close despite her dripping wet. "Your suit is getting soaked."

"It will dry. Thank God you are home." He hugged her tight and kissed her shoulder before grabbing the towel from the rail and wrapping her in it. "I don't want you getting a chill. Would you like dinner in bed or do you want to come downstairs?"

"I'll eat with the family. I missed them." Kathleen wrapped her hair in a towel before getting dressed in fresh clothes. "We are so lucky Richard. All night I kept thinking about Esme and Max, they are of similar age. What if we hadn't adopted Esme after the General Slocum? She could have ended up on the streets just like…"

He put his arms around her holding her close as she finally let the tears flow.

# CHAPTER 7

*N*ettie stayed with them for two nights, sharing Esme's bedroom. Esme found some of her old clothes, and the girls had great fun playing dress-up. Max continued to improve at the hospital. Every time Kathleen went to visit him, she found Miss Cooper in his room.

"Dr. Green suggested I help look after him. He needs someone watching him all the time," Miss Cooper's cheeks turned red as she jumped up from the chair when Kathleen arrived.

Kathleen smiled, "Please sit back down. You are doing a wonderful job. Richard has been singing your praises."

A look of disbelief clouded the girl's eyes, but when she saw Kathleen meant it, she smiled, a smile that lit up her whole face. "I don't do much. Just sit with him to make sure he doesn't try to get out of bed again. He had a few nightmares. He keeps calling for Nettie, and I have to reassure him she is safe and well."

Kathleen took a seat by the bed, her hand pushing Max's hair back from his eyes. "He's been through so much. Is he still sleeping all the time?"

"He's been waking up more and staying awake for a little while. I told him Nettie was staying with you and that you would bring her in to visit when he was better. He asked what was going to happen to them, you know, when he gets out of here." Miss Cooper played with her fingers before speaking in a whisper. "He asked me to promise they wouldn't separate him and Nettie. But I couldn't do that." Miss Cooper looked up and held Kathleen's gaze. "We both know they keep boys and girls in different parts of the orphanages. It's the same all over, isn't it?"

"In the big ones, yes. But I hope to avoid that with these children. I have a sister who runs an orphanage in Riverside Springs. I also know some people who are involved in the Orphan Trains. I hope to find them a home together."

"You aren't going to keep them, then?"

Kathleen stood up and walked to the window, looking out at the street outside. There was still some snow on the ground, but it didn't look pretty now that several people had walked through it. Instead of being white, it had turned into a dark grey sludge.

"I'm sorry, I shouldn't have asked."

Miss Cooper's words brought her back to the room. She turned. "I'd love to take them. Richard and I have discussed it, but now isn't the right time. Richard is so busy with the new burns unit, and I have a lot of responsibility with my work at Carmel's Mission. My friends, Lily and Charlie, are away on an extended vacation, so I need to be there. I have another orphan family of five depending on me." Kathleen held out her hands. "I just can't do it. I wish I could." She turned back to the window, but not quickly enough.

"Mrs. Green, please don't cry. You have done so much already. Too many people would have walked away and let the policeman arrest this poor boy, and then where would he have ended up." Miss Cooper put her arm around Kathleen's waist and drew her to the chair. "You sit with Max for a bit, and I'll go find you some coffee. How do you like it? Cream and sugar?"

Kathleen nodded, too choked up to speak. The door closed softly behind the young girl, leaving Kathleen and Max alone.

Kathleen edged the seat closer to the bed. "I swear, Max, if I could, I would give you and Nettie a home. But it's just not possible."

It wasn't just for the reasons she had given Miss Cooper. Richard had confided he was worried about the effect having two more children would have on their existing children. Little Richie and Esme had to get used to living without Patrick and Frieda, both of whom had played a large role in their short lives. Esme was particularly close to Frieda and missed her dreadfully. Adding two more orphaned children to the family might not be in their best interests. Richard had also suggested that when Max was ready to leave, he go straight to the sanctuary. They would move Nettie to the sanctuary soon too. Carrie and the other Chiver children would welcome her, and at least Esme may not become too attached.

Kathleen watched the young boy's chest rise and fall, wondering why life had to be so complicated. Her thoughts flew back to the letters she'd exchanged with her sister. Bridget would never turn children away, even with her financial issues, but it would be best for everyone if she could find a family willing to take in these two precious children.

# CHAPTER 8

$\mathcal{L}$ily held Charlie's hand as their horse-drawn cab made its way from the port down through Sackville Street. The Dublin streets, wet from the recent rain, now sparkled in the faint sunshine. People walked along the paths in front of the stores; nobody seemed to be in a particular hurry. It was so different from New York and London.

They'd had an enjoyable week in London, helping Frieda and Patrick settle into their new home. Lily and Frieda enjoyed shopping while Charlie did more sightseeing. Leaving their friends behind in London had been difficult. Charlie suggested taking a few days to travel from London to Liverpool, where they had taken the boat to Dublin. Lily was glad to be back on firm ground after the rough Irish Sea.

The cab drew up outside a small hotel, their home for the next week. The cab driver held out his hand to assist Lily from the cab before fetching their trunks. She stared at the modest sign bearing the hotel's name, Hayfield House, above the entrance to a moderately sized four-story building. Built in 1855, its ornate stonework and large windows gave it a sense of grandeur. She took Charlie's arm as he escorted her up the steps and through into the well-lit, cozy lobby adorned with dark wooden paneling and floral-patterned wallpapers. A plush Persian rug covered the polished wooden floor, her heels sinking into it as she made her way to the wooden reception desk. A large chandelier hung from the ceiling, with additional lights dotted along the walls.

The concierge greeted them with a smile as a bellboy appeared with their luggage.

"Mr. and Mrs. Doherty, welcome to our hotel. I trust you will find things to your satisfaction. Please let us know if you have any requests. Is this your first time in Dublin?"

"Yes, it is. My wife and I intend to go to the west to visit my family home, but first, we wish to spend a week relaxing and doing a little sightseeing."

"We will be very happy to help with suggestions of what to see, where to eat, and how to travel. If you could just sign here, please, Mr. Doherty."

The concierge took a room key from the brass key rack behind him before he turned the ledger book around for Charlie to sign. Once signed, the key was passed over, and the concierge directed the bellboy to take the luggage to room 337.

They took the stairs to the third floor. Charlie turned the key and stood back to let Lily enter first. "Oh, Charlie, look, it's so pretty." The room was warm and inviting, with a fire lit in the small fireplace. A four-poster bed took pride of place against one wall, while the wall opposite was composed of windows looking over Sackville Street. Each window had heavy floral drapes held back with a rope, so they could be drawn closed if guests wanted privacy. A washbasin with pitcher and basin stood beside the mahogany closet. A writing desk with quill and inkwell sat under one of the windows. It was very quaint and old-fashioned compared to what they were used to at home. A second door led to a small water closet.

"Would you like to eat in the hotel tonight, darling?"

"I think I'd prefer to sleep. That crossing was so rough, my stomach still hasn't settled, and that bed looks so comfortable. It is like something a queen would lie on."

Charlie smiled at her comment. "I'm glad to see you smiling. If you want to have a nap, I shall leave you in peace."

"What will you do?"

"I want to explore a little. Patrick bought me a guidebook in London, so I will have a look around."

"But I want to see Dublin too."

"We will go exploring tomorrow. For now, relax. Will I ring for some refreshments?"

She shook her head. There was fresh water and a glass by the bed. That was all she needed for now.

After a wonderful night's sleep and a lovely filling traditional Irish breakfast with rashers, sausages, pudding, potato cakes, and brown bread, Lily was ready to explore the city. On the advice of the concierge, as Lily was still feeling a little tired and not up for lots of walking, they decided to take the tram out to the seaside village of Howth.

"Charlie, what is that?" Lily pointed to a towering cylindrical shaft with fluted sides, topped by a bronze statue.

"Nelson's Pillar. I read about it in my guidebook. It's 134 feet tall, constructed of granite. The statue is of Admiral Horatio Nelson, the same man from the statue in Trafalgar Square in London."

"Was he Irish? Is that why this is here?"

Lily's question caused a passerby to laugh. "No, love, he wasn't Irish, but he was a great naval officer. They stuck him here, so we'd all remember him, is my guess."

Lily stared after the man who kept walking before exchanging an amused look with Charlie.

"Well, at least we can't get lost. We just need to head for this statue, and we will find the hotel. I think that's our tram coming. Watch out, Lily." Charlie pulled her out of the way of a horse and cart.

They boarded the tram, taking a seat on the wooden benches. As the tram departed, they were able to take in the sights. "That's the General Post Office, over there. We should get some stamps and send some letters to the family and Kathleen. She is bound to be missing you."

Lily didn't want to think about Kathleen or the Sanctuary. Not that she didn't miss her friends, but thinking of New York made her think of the fire and everything else. She fixed her smile in place, not wanting Charlie to know he had reminded her. He pointed out places of interest from his guidebook as the tram moved along the streets. Lily watched as local children, some barefoot, ran across the streets, dodging the traffic as they sold papers, or shouted for boots and shoes to be cleaned. Female traders sold fruit and vegetables from their stalls on some streets, while on others, only stores were visible. The conductor called out the names of stops along the way, as the tram continued through the North Strand area, passing by rows of shops and terraced houses. As the tram made its way, they passed through the more affluent area of Clontarf with larger houses and cleaner streets. Here, there were no signs of raggedly clothed children or female traders. Instead, they spotted ladies in well-made dresses accompanied by gentlemen in coats and hats. As they traveled, the scenery became progressively coastal, with them spotting sailing boats in the sea. They didn't see anyone swimming; Lily guessed it was probably too cold, as she burrowed her hands into the pockets of her heavy coat. The salty air stung her cheeks. The stunning views from Howth made the trip worthwhile, with an enjoyable fresh seafood lunch at a lovely restaurant up on the cliffs overlooking the harbor.

"Isn't this so beautiful?"

Lily smiled at Charlie. He looked more relaxed than she had seen him in a long time.

"Does it feel different from England?"

He nodded. "You will probably tell me I'm being silly, but part of me feels like I have come home. This is the country of my ancestors; it seems to have a pull on my heart or something." He pushed his hair back from his eyes in a gesture of self-consciousness. She leaned in and kissed him. "I don't think it is silly at all. A feeling of belonging is important. To all of us."

After a lovely week sightseeing, they decided to return to Howth for their last day in Dublin before heading west. It was March 17th, St. Patrick's Day. But there was no parade in Dublin City, something Lily found odd given the annual parade in New York.

"Are ye visiting or do you live here?"

Lily started, not seeing the man who had spoken as he was sitting on a stone ledge beside the quay, his nets and a hook in his hands. Decades of exposure to harsh salty winds, sun, and the elements had etched deep wrinkles into his leathery brown skin. His eyes twinkled with life as he looked up and smiled.

"We're visiting. Over from New York."

"That's a fine city. I've been there a couple of times. Always nice to visit." The man gestured to the seat beside him. "Will you take a seat? You look rather windblown."

As if listening to him, the wind had another go at removing Lily's hat from her head. Laughing, she put her hand up to stop the hat from escaping and gratefully sat down.

"You're not visiting alone, are ye?"

"No, my husband is over there. He fancied walking to the very end of the quay. He wanted to watch the boats, but this was far enough for me. It's such a beautiful spot." Lily gazed up at the mountains overlooking the harbor, thinking what a fabulous view a house built up there would have.

"No better place than Ireland. 'Tis God's sacred country. It has everything you could wish for and lots more."

Lily glanced at his nets and the small boat moored nearest to them.

"What do you fish for?"

"A bit of Cod and Haddock when I'm lucky, but mostly it's Whiting. During the summer, there's plenty of Mackerel about, but they don't like the cold waters of this time of year. So, what brings you to Ireland?"

"My husband's family came from Sligo originally. They left after the famine in 1852. He wanted to see where they lived."

The man coughed before lighting up a pipe, discarding the net and hook to one side.

"That was a dreadful business. All those men, women, and children heading to America on the coffin ships. They called them that because so many died on board, they never got to see land. But it must have been good for your husband's family for ye to be able to come back. Most don't. If they are lucky, they send a few dollars back every so often to the ones left behind on the land."

Lily wasn't sure Carmel would have considered her early life in New York to be lucky, but she didn't comment about that. "My husband's grandmother is still living. She moved out of New York and is living in Colorado now. She writes to say the village reminds her a little of Ireland. She's too old to make the journey home. She turns eighty in a few weeks' time."

The man smiled. "That's a great age to live, even if you are away from home. My family were lucky in the famine, most of Dublin didn't suffer as much as those in the country. We had our boats, and we could fish as much as we wanted. We had enough to share too. My grandparents used to barter their catch with those who had other things like flour or sugar or whatnot. The community came together and looked after those who needed help."

The man picked up the hook and moved it

through the net as he spoke. "Although as time went by, I believe the country folk who could walk, walked to Dublin to find work. My parents and their parents used to talk about the crowds of starving people milling about on the roads. It was difficult in Dublin, but there were many of the big houses full of the English so folks had employment. Some of those big houses set up soup kitchens to help feed the people. Not all English people behaved badly, regardless of what you hear. People are the same the world over, some good, some bad, most trying to be the best they can."

"You are a wise man, Mr. …"

"Michael is the name."

"Nice to meet you, Michael. My name is Lily Doherty, and my husband is called Charlie."

"What have you seen so far, Miss Lily?"

Lily thought about all the sights she had seen. "I think my favorite was St. Patrick's Cathedral. My husband wanted to go to church, I don't usually attend, but I did on Sunday. There was a choir, and I think they sounded like you imagine angels would. It was so beautiful, and of course, the church was magnificent. It was packed full of people too, from all walks of life. It was an experience I won't forget."

When Michael remained silent, Lily continued. "We visited Trinity College and the Royal College of Surgeons, but I preferred the Phoenix Park. It is so big; you couldn't walk that in a single day. We saw deer and lots of other wildlife, and it was so peaceful. It was wonderful. We had lunch in a pretty village called Chapelizod. It's on the River Liffey. Do you know it?"

"I've heard of it, but I haven't been out there. Now, is that your man coming? That wind is rising, and you will turn blue with the cold with what little you are wearing." The old man stood up, his stooped shoulders highlighting the years at sea. Charlie reached them, and Lily made the introductions.

Michael asked, "Have you eaten yet?"

"Not since breakfast."

"Good. Then let me take you to the best fish dinner you will find this side of the Shannon. Come along now." Michael offered her his elbow, and she took it, exchanging a smile with Charlie.

Michael took them to a small pub with a room they called the snug, where ladies were welcome. They took a seat opposite the large turf-filled open fire. After the bitterly cold wind, Lily was grateful. Michael disappeared and returned with two pints of black liquid with a frothy cream top and a small glass for Lily. "Guinness for the men and a small glass of Irish whiskey for the lady. Sláinte."

Lily tried a sip of the whiskey, but it was far too rich for her blood. She'd have been happy with water. Michael drank his pint as if it was the first liquid he'd seen for years. Charlie drank his more slowly as Michael ordered more drinks. Luckily, Lily caught the waiter's eye and asked for some water. Michael told them stories of his trips to different places, and then the food arrived. It was a simple fish stew, but it was delicious. Hunks of fresh brown bread accompanied it, served with butter as high as doorsteps. As they ate, someone picked up a tin whistle and played some haunting Irish music. Then another man picked up an accordion, and the tempo turned more lively. A customer started to sing, and soon everyone joined in. Then they started dancing.

Lily gasped as the dancing got faster and faster, the room spinning as she moved from one partner to another. Pleading sore feet, she apologized to her partner and went back to sit down.

"Your husband is light on his feet. He looks like he's been dancing for years," Michael put another drink down in front of Lily.

Lily smiled her thanks. "He thinks he's still in his twenties." Despite her remark, it was lovely to see her husband letting his hair down and enjoying himself. The last few years had been tough on him. He'd been her rock, but who'd supported him through everything? She laughed as he twirled a young woman around and around. The musicians picked up the beat as the dancers took up the challenge, everyone moving whether it was on the dance floor or those tapping their feet as they sat out the dance.

"Do you go to the Céilidh in New York? Is that where he learned the dancing?" Michael asked.

"No, at least not with me. I don't know if he went before we met."

Drinks flowed as Michael told the locals

about the Dohertys coming home to find the home of their grandparents. Everyone was so friendly, asking questions, and making suggestions as to what trips they should take and places they must see on their way to Sligo and back. All too soon, it was time to leave as they had to catch the last tram back into Dublin.

"Thank you so much for your hospitality, Michael. We had a wonderful day."

"You are very welcome, lovely Lily. A rare prize you have there, Mr. Doherty. A good-looking woman who doesn't talk too much and allows her man to enjoy a decent drink."

Lily couldn't look at Charlie as they left. Only once they were outside and out of earshot did they laugh. "I think that's the only time in my life anyone will ever say I have a quiet woman as a wife."

Lily raised her eyebrows, but Charlie quickly continued. "I love you just the way you are, Lily Doherty. From the first day I set eyes on you, you took my breath away then and every day since."

## CHAPTER 9

Kathleen, Emily, Gustav, Conrad, and Father Nelson sat in Lily's office as they discussed the plans for the next few weeks, including what would happen to the children currently living in the sanctuary. Ethel knocked at the door before entering with a large tray of refreshments.

"Thank you, Ethel, just leave it on the table. Please pass on our thanks to Cook as well," Kathleen smiled at the maid, who still looked very nervous despite being in her role for several weeks. Ethel bobbed a curtsey and fled.

"How are things going at the factory?" Father Nelson reached over to help himself to a plate and a selection of sandwiches.

"Good. The orders are coming in at last, and the women are busy. Conrad is training some new cutters. The men aren't happy as he is training a woman too, but..." Gustav shrugged his shoulders, "the boss is a woman, so they might as well get used to new things."

"With Lily, they will be kept on their toes," Emily smiled sweetly at her husband, who blushed charmingly.

"Emily, how is the classroom working? Do you have enough help?"

Emily had blossomed since her marriage and taking up the role of teacher at the factory. It had been Lily's idea to add a room where the children who were not yet in school could stay while their parents worked in the factory. Emily looked after the children, teaching English to those old enough or bright enough. Most of their workforce were immigrants who were often illiterate. She also taught English to some of the seamstresses who came to see their children during their lunch hours. Lily insisted all staff had an hour for lunch. Their workday began at eight in the morning and finished at six, regardless of whether they had reached their targets or not.

Other shirtwaist factory owners had laughed, stating the workforce would take advantage of Lily's kindness, but the opposite had proven true. The staff reached their targets, and the work they produced was of the best quality. They seemed to appreciate being treated properly. There were no locked doors and no searches made of anyone on leaving the property. Gustav was a strict master in that the factory floor was kept clean and free of rubbish, all recommendations made by the fire marshal were followed. Fire drills were conducted every month, and nobody was allowed to skip them. The workers grumbled, particularly when the drills meant they had to congregate in the rain at the appointed meeting point. But Gustav took no notice. The safety of the workforce meant everything to him.

"Is there anything you need for the factory?" Kathleen addressed both Gustav and Conrad. They worked well together.

"We will soon need to hire more workers if the orders keep coming. We may need more space soon," Conrad spoke up, his eyes lit up with excitement. "We are turning away workers at the moment; seems word is spreading that our factory is the place to work."

Kathleen pushed her hair back from her eyes. "That's good news, but let's wait until Lily gets back before we expand much further." Kathleen was struggling to keep on top of her workload as it was.

Conrad nodded his agreement, his mouth full of cake.

"We need to appoint a new agent to take the children on the train to Riverside Springs. I have letters here from people Bridget knows who are willing to adopt the children. Bridget assures me she has interviewed every couple, and they are all decent people. One family will take Max and Nettie, so we don't need to worry about them being split up." Father Nelson pushed the papers to one side, eyeing Kathleen. When she didn't answer, he took another drink of his tea and helped himself to a slice of cake.

Kathleen dreaded saying goodbye to Nettie and Max. She and Richard had spoken about adopting them, but it wasn't the right time. Richard was busy at the hospital, she had the sanctuary to run, and the children needed lots of love and attention and a fresh start. New York would always hold painful memories.

She wished she could travel with them and see her sister and brother as well as her nieces and nephews, but with Lily in Ireland, it wasn't practical. She was needed at the sanctuary.

"I met someone I think would be highly suitable, but you might need to work your magic, Father Nelson."

"Why?"

"Miss Cooper currently works as a skivvy at the hospital. She looked after Nettie the night Max was admitted. She is kind and very capable and would be perfect."

"But?"

"She's an orphan currently living in the New York Asylum."

Father Nelson put his cup back on the saucer.

"I don't see the problem. What am I missing?"

"I imagine the Asylum is getting paid for her work at the hospital, and I sense Matron may be reluctant to let her go. I can't be seen to get involved, not with Richard working at the hospital." Kathleen looked Father Nelson in the eye. "Miss Cooper believes as an orphan she should be grateful for her position in the hospital. She has been working there since she was twelve, starting in the kitchens and working her way up to being a ward cleaner. She's bright and amazingly cheerful, particularly given her circumstances. I know she's young, but I believe she would be perfect to accompany the children. Nettie and Max both know her; she spent hours of her own time with Max keeping him company when he was in the hospital. Bridget wrote that there is a shortage of young single women in Riverside Springs, so I believe she could make a life for herself there."

"Is it a matchmaking service you're running?" Father Nelson had a twinkle in his eye.

"Just thinking ahead. As Lily said before, if all the single men in Riverside Springs and the surrounding areas were to get married, that creates more family units who may offer homes to our orphans."

# CHAPTER 10

*C*harlie offered Lily his hand to help her out of the carriage once the train finally came to a stop at Sligo station. Smoke billowed from the steam engine, blocking her view, and the disembarking passengers crowded onto the platform, all heading for the same exit. Porters blew their whistles while relatives or friends greeted the new arrivals. Lily glanced at her husband's face. He was both excited and terrified at what they might find. After all the years of listening to his grandmother's stories, he was finally here in the county where she had been born.

She squeezed his hand, reminding him that she was traveling the journey with him; he was not alone. A young man in his late twenties, dressed in a tweed jacket patched in several places, a cotton shirt, and woolen trousers with fraying hems, moved to their side, swiping his cap from his head. "Newly arrived from Dublin and strangers to the area, I'm guessing. Do you need lodgings for the night? Would you like me to take your bags? I have a wagon outside." He ran his other hand through his chestnut curls, perhaps hoping to make a good impression, but the hair remained tousled. His eyes, a deep blue, sparkled with mischief and good humor, his smile warm and welcoming. Lily guessed most people liked this young man.

"Thank you, but we have secured local lodgings at O'Reilly's guesthouse. A man we met in Dublin recommended it. Do you know it?"

"Ah, to be sure, don't we all know it? Widow O'Reilly serves the best breakfast in the whole of Ireland. Tis but a short walk from here. I would have recommended it myself, but I thought youse may have required more salubrious surroundings. Given how you are dressed for high society like." Before Charlie could answer, the man continued, "Have you more bags, or are you traveling light?"

Charlie glanced at Lily. "We have a small trunk. The porter said he'd bring it to the waiting room."

"Was it Paddy or Liam you were dealing with?"

Lily had to turn to hide her smile. Did everyone in Ireland know one another? When Charlie didn't answer fast enough, the man said, "Sure, it's hardly relevant. I'll go find your trunk, and you take your good lady to the waiting room. I'll catch up with you in a minute."

"Wait, I don't even know your name."

"Seamus, Seamus Flynn, but everyone calls me Flynty. My father's a blacksmith, and I grew up in the Smithy helping him. My elder brothers have followed him into the trade, but not me. Far too hot and sweaty, although I love the horses. I prefer to turn my hand at this and that. I love talking to people, so I take people like yourselves wherever they like to go. We get a lot of tourists, although not usually this early in the year. Many Americans and Canadians coming back to the land of their birth or that of their grandfathers. I know the area like the back of my hand, so I do. It's a great job, but sometimes the weather can be nasty. Like earlier today with the wet rain."

Lily couldn't help herself. "Wet rain?"

"Aye, missus. That's the rain that runs down the back of your neck no matter what you be wearing. Tis hits you from every side, and you get as wet as a dog out on the bog. But it's passed now, and the sun is shining. Ready to give you a warm Sligo welcome." He grinned, revealing a mouth missing several teeth. "You go on now and find a seat, and leave everything to me."

Charlie offered Lily his arm once more as they made their way to the waiting room. As she glanced around, she knew why Flynty knew they were outsiders. It wasn't just their accents; it was their clothes. There were few women in the station aside from the newly arrived passengers, and most wore ankle-length skirts made from durable fabrics.

They sat in the crowded waiting room, watching the large clock. Several minutes passed, and there was no sign of Flynty. Charlie picked up a discarded newspaper while

Lily continued her people watching, letting her thoughts drift. They planned to stay in Sligo for a week. Today they would rest after traveling, and tomorrow they would explore the town, taking in a few of the historical sights. The next day, Charlie hoped to head to the townland where Carmel Doherty had once lived. Carmel had written to them from Clover Springs, enclosing a small hand-drawn map to help them locate her former home and the graveyard where her grandparents were buried. Her own parents had been buried in a mass grave during the famine. There was no marker for them or the thousands of others who'd died. Carmel had mentioned some extended family members who may still live in the area, but she'd also written to say they too may have emigrated. She didn't write to anyone in Ireland. There was no one left of her family, and her connection with the Dohertys had died with Joseph. Lily had shed a tear reading Carmel's letter, sensing the longing the old lady had to see her home once more. Now that they had traveled here and found it not too onerous, maybe they would be able to persuade Carmel to take the trip.

"Doherty, Charlie Doherty."

Charlie stood up at the shout and, with a wave at Flynty, turned to Lily. "I thought he had absconded with our trunk." Lily smiled as she took her husband's arm. They were too used to the fast-paced life of New York. Dublin had moved at a slower pace, and she sensed down here in the country, things moved slower still.

They walked out of the station to find Flynty standing by a horse and trap. The horse looked well cared for, and a fresh rug had been laid across the seat to protect Lily's dress from the rain.

"Take a seat, and I'll drive you over to Widow O'Reilly's."

"I thought it was within walking distance."

"It is, to be sure, but your good lady's shoes will get destroyed. Better we let Daisy take us."

Charlie climbed up first. Lily took Flynty's outstretched hand and allowed him to help her onto the seat. She guessed he needed the fare more than he let on.

The horse plodded at a sedate pace as Flynty fired questions at them.

"Are you here for a holiday or in search of yer roots?"

"A bit of both. My grandparents emigrated after the famine and settled in New York. My grandmother told me a lot about her home, and we finally decided it was time to come visit."

"Tis a pity you couldn't have waited for the summer. At least then you'd have a better chance of getting some sun on yer backs." Flynty wiped his nose on his sleeve before continuing. "Where were your grandparents from?"

"My gran was from a place called Trenton's Field . Do you know it?"

"Aye, sure every child around here could direct you there. Are you heading out that way today?"

"No. We planned to take a day or so to rest. We traveled from New York to Southampton, from there to London, and then over to Dublin, so we are quite exhausted."

Lily watched the way Flynty's face fell at Charlie's comment. She spoke up.

"We'd like to visit in a couple of days. Would you be free to take us?"

His eyes lit up. "Aye, sure, I will make myself available. Daisy likes the sea air, so she does. I'll borrow the carriage in case it rains. Or snows." Flynty pulled gently on the horse's reins. "This is us."

Lily glanced at the guesthouse. It was slightly bigger than the houses around it, but that wasn't the only difference. Curtains adorned the tall slash windows either side of the heavy paneled front door. The roof wasn't thatched like most but tiled with dark slate, with an elegant chimney from which smoke billowed into the sky. Dormer windows broke through the roofline; was that where they would sleep? She imagined the views would be incredible, although her husband, being a tall man, might find the height restrictive. The walled-in front garden was carefully mani-cured with rose bushes decorating either side of the gravel path leading to the front door.

Flynty jumped down before holding out his hand to help her. She descended as delicately as she could, but her skirt caught on something; she wobbled and would have fallen but for him putting his hands on her waist and lifting her down. His actions caused her to blush, but he didn't seem to notice. She walked around the horse to Charlie's side. Flynty declined help, lifting their trunk on one shoulder as if it were a small bag.

"I'll take this round the back. Widow O'Reilly doesn't take kindly to the likes of me using her front door. You ring the bell, although she probably spied you from the window."

Whistling, he walked away, around the back of the house and out of sight. Daisy chewed contentedly on some grass by the roadside, leaving Charlie and Lily to wander up the path alone. Charlie was about to ring the bell when it opened, and a beaming woman with greying hair tied up in a bun greeted them. "The Dohertys, I take it. I was expecting you earlier."

Lily found herself apologizing, but the woman waved them away. "Come away inside, you're letting the heat out. Fierce weather we've been having, but that's March for you. Come along, right through here; this is the main sitting room. All my guests share it. Are ye hungry, or would you like a cup of tea first?" The woman was talking so fast with a heavy accent, Lily found her quite hard to follow.

Charlie answered for them, "Something to eat would be wonderful, Mrs. O'Reilly, if that isn't too much trouble. It's been a long time since breakfast."

"'Tis no trouble at all. Let me show you to your room first; you may want to wash up. I'll set dinner up in the dining room. There is nobody staying at present, so you shall have it all to yourselves."

They followed the woman up the stairs, the walls adorned with portraits of people, perhaps family members. The high ceilings made the house look bigger, the cream-colored walls adding an element of warmth. Mrs. O'Reilly opened the door to a bedroom and ushered them inside.

"This is beautiful, thank you," Lily exclaimed as she surveyed the room. The large double bed was covered in a beautiful lace-edged bedspread with matching pillows. A water jug, bowl, and some towels sat above the brown chest of drawers in one corner of the room. A matching closet occupied the other. Their trunk and small traveling bag were sitting next to the closet.

"I'll leave you to it. The dining room is the

second door on the right when you come down the stairs. I'll have the meal on the table in fifteen minutes." With that, Mrs. O'Reilly disappeared.

Lily sat on the edge of the bed. The mattress was soft as a feather cloud; she wished she could forgo lunch and just sleep. Charlie stared out the window at the view.

# CHAPTER 11

*C*harlie pushed back from the table, his hands resting on his stomach. "I can't remember when I have ever felt so full. Gran was right, there is nothing like an Irish potato." Just then, the door opened and Mrs. O'Reilly arrived with a tray carrying a teapot, some cups, a jug of milk, and a large cake.

Charlie leapt to his feet to help her. "'Tis reared well you were, young man. I can manage, but thank you kindly. Did I hear you saying your gran liked Irish potatoes?"

"She did. She came from near here but left after the famine."

"The Gorta Mór." The woman crossed herself. Then she lifted the lid of the teapot and gave it a stir before pouring it into the cups.

"Do you mind if I join ye in a cup of tea? I thought we could get to know one another a little bit."

"We'd love that. Lily is sick of listening to me going on," Charlie grinned at her.

"'Tis a common enough name, Doherty. Where did you say your grandmother was from?"

"A place called Trenton's Field . Do ye know it?"

"Aye. It's only a little bit out the road." Mrs. O'Reilly took a sip of her tea.

"Flinty said he would take us the day after tomorrow."

Widow O'Reilly nodded. "I bet he did. Now don't get me wrong, Flinty is a nice young man, but 'tis my Frank you be needing. He knows everyone 'round hereabouts. I dare say he knew your grandmother too."

Charlie leaned into the table. "Do you think he might? Where would I find him? I'd love to ask him a few questions."

The widow stood up. "Cut yourself a large slice of the cake. I'll be right back."

She came back with an elderly, stooped gentleman, his back curved from a lifetime of working in the fields. His hands were gnarled and rough with calluses but surprisingly strong for his age, as Lily winced when he took her fingers in his. He nearly shook Charlie's arm off.

"Maeve says you're a Doherty from the point. What was your grandfather's name, my boyo?"

"Joseph, sir."

"Joseph Doherty, well as I live and breathe it. I thought so as soon as I set eyes on ye. You have the look of that line of Doherty's. Patrick, he was a good friend of mine. Well, until he stole my girl away. Carmel Curran, with eyes the color of sapphires, she was a beauty, so she was. And wise too. Beyond her years. Didn't take any sass from anyone, did Carmel."

"She still doesn't. But according to my gran, there was only ever one man for her. I never met my grandfather, but Gran told me all about him."

Frank sat down as Maeve set a cup of tea and a slice of cake in front of him. He nodded his thanks, but his eyes never left Charlie's.

"'Tis true. As soon as she laid eyes on Joseph Doherty, it was as if the rest of us men ceased to exist. She was my one true love."

Lily could have listened to the old man all day, the tone of his voice making his words come out like a song. Despite his age, he had spirit.

Maeve elbowed him. "Ah, go on with you. She was not. You had a one true love in every township from here to Cork. And the women knew it too. If this Carmel woman had any brains at all, she'd have steered well clear of you, you old goat."

Lily sputtered as the tea caught the back of her throat. Maeve handed her a napkin. "Sorry about that, love, but he gets ideas about himself. Always has done. The babe of the family and his mother, God Rest her Soul, had him destroyed. She reared him to believe the perfect woman for him hadn't been born, and her mother was dead." Maeve roared laughing as Frank grinned, his eyes twinkling, not the least bit insulted. It was clear that these two had a good relationship despite the teasing going on between them.

"You didn't know Charlie's grandparents then, Mrs. O'Reilly."

"No, lass, I didn't. I'm not from 'round hereabouts. I grew up in Knock – you may have heard of it as the Blessed Virgin appeared there." She waited to see their reaction, but neither replied. She shrugged and continued. "I didn't move to Sligo town until I met my Patrick, Frank's older and nicer brother. He was working in a store over in Knock to get experience, and then he came back here, and we bought a small store. He lived for that shop, so he did."

Frank patted Maeve's hand as the widow put her hanky to her eyes.

"I'm very sorry for your loss, Mrs. O'Reilly."

Frank winked at Lily. "Ah sure, he's been dead for longer than they were ever married, but she needs to keep up appearances. He left her well provided for." He eyed up the room as if seeing it for the first time.

Lily opened her mouth to reply, but Maeve got there first. "Francis Joseph Mary O'Reilly, as I live and breathe, you can find yourself somewhere else to eat if that's the way you are going to talk to me. Your poor brother would be turning in his grave." Maeve turned to Lily. "I was an only child, and my parents were quite well off. They gave me a good dowry, and we bought a shop. Patrick died two years after we were married. A delivery came to the store, and a child ran out; would have been killed if Patrick hadn't grabbed the poor thing out of the way. Got a kick in the head from the horse for his trouble. He was dead before he hit the ground. It was a long time ago, as Frank said, but I never looked at another man."

Frank took out a pipe and pushed some tobacco into it. "Ya did so, but they ran a mile."

"You... oh, why do I invite you for tea when you talk like this?"

"'Cause you love me like a brother." Frank blew her a kiss, and despite her remarks, she laughed.

Lily liked this odd couple.

The next morning, Frank arrived early to take them on the promised tour of the area. The first place they visited was the old Abbey. As Lily walked through the gates of Sligo Abbey, her eyes drank in the contrast of the ancient ruins and the teeming buildings she had left behind in New York. For the first time since the fire, her mind stilled as she let the peaceful atmosphere wash over her. She fell behind Frank and Charlie, who were chatting about families and connections, allowing the thousands of years of history to wash over her. Maeve told her the Abbey had been a Dominican Friary built sometime in the 13th century, and as she trailed across the path, her fingers touching the cold rough stones, she imagined the monks in silent prayer toiling away within these surroundings. There was nothing left of the roof; as you looked up, all you could see was the clear sky. The light filtered through what remained of the windows, casting shadows on the ground. She stepped into the nave, or heart of the Abbey, allowing the tranquility of her surroundings to soothe her soul.

Her gaze was drawn to the intricately carved high altar, still standing in defiance of the years. The stone was etched with gothic designs, figures of saints and angels that once were painted in vibrant hues, now a ghostly grey. It had survived fires, wars, and neglect. Among the remains, she found the cloister, imagining the monks walking along these same paths as they meditated. She stopped for a few seconds, imagining she could hear whispers on the wind carrying their prayers from bygone centuries.

"Are you alright there, Mrs. Doherty? Your face is the color of milk?"

Lily jumped at Frank's voice. She hadn't noticed him walk back to her.

"I was just thinking of the history of this place. I don't think we have any buildings in New York as old as this. It's overwhelming to think about what different times the people who used to live around the Abbey have been through."

Frank rubbed his whiskered face. "Aye, good times and bad, to be sure. Given it's a grand day, a bit windy but dry like, I thought you might like to see the sea. Would that suit you? Blow away the cobwebs and put a bit of color in your cheeks." He held out his arm, and she took it, part reluctant to leave this place but also part relieved.

Lily gazed at the countryside around her, trying but failing to find words to describe its raw beauty. It seemed like a cliché, but the grass was greener, and the water bluer, and the stormy purple-streaked sky just added to the magical effect.

"Can you imagine having to leave here knowing you would never see it again?" Charlie whispered, gripping her hand tighter.

"Look at that sea, Charlie. The waves are so powerful; it takes your breath away." Lily inhaled the salt-scented air. They couldn't see anything but water for miles. When she turned her back on the ocean view, she saw the mountains behind her.

"WHAT'S THAT?" she asked him, pointing to a mound barely visible through a break in the clouds atop one of them.

"Binn Ghulbain – or as the English call it, Benbulbin. 'Tis supposed to be Gráinne and Diarmuid's final resting place."

"Were they members of your family?"

The old man laughed so much, Lily feared for his safety as his face turned purple. The laughter turned into a fit of coughing, only ending when Charlie whacked Frank on his back.

"I shouldn't be laughing. No, they aren't

family, but rather two young lovers from stories passed down to us by the seanachai."

"Who?"

"The seanachai. They are men with the gift of storytelling. In the old days, they used to travel from one area to another, telling their stories in return for a bed, a decent meal, and a drop of whiskey, or failing that, poitín if there was any to be had. In ancient myths, the old King of Ireland – Cormac MacAirt – promised his young daughter in marriage to Fionn MacCool, a man of a similar age to himself. Gráinne fell in love with a younger man, a warrior by the name of Diarmuid. The wedding arrangements between Gráinne and Fionn were very advanced, and everyone knew there would be bloodshed if it was called off. Gráinne didn't care; she wanted Diarmuid. She put a spell on all the guests to make them fall asleep and another one on Diarmuid to make him run away with her, him being a bit reluctant like."

Lily exchanged a look with Charlie. "As usual, the woman gets all the blame in these old stories. It doesn't seem to matter whether they are told in America or here in Ireland; the woman is always at fault."

Old Frank shrugged his shoulders. "Sure, 'tis well known that a beautiful woman will bring trouble. Haven't you heard of Helen of Troy?" The man wiped his nose with his sleeve. "Have you seen enough, or would you like to start walking back? I've a thirst on me worse than any traveler in the desert."

Lily wanted to stay, but she saw Charlie was keen to humor the old man who had ties to his family. They turned and walked back in the direction of the town.

"Why are there so many small walls?" Lily asked.

"That was what they had us doing during the famine. Building walls and roads to nowhere. The poor creatures could barely put one foot in front of the other, but they had to work or they wouldn't get paid. And the few pennies they earned building these walls and roads was the difference between life and death. For many, it was too little, too late."

Lily wished she hadn't asked. The famine. Wasn't that what Carmel had blamed for her and Joseph leaving Ireland? She should have asked Charlie's grandmother more about it when she had the chance.

They returned to the town. Charlie walked Lily to the door of the guesthouse. "Are you sure you don't want me to stay with you, darling?"

She rubbed his arm before leaning in to kiss his cheek. "Go and see what Frank can tell you about Carmel's history. All this fresh air is making me tired. I think I will have a nap."

Charlie hesitated, but she gave him a small push. "Go on. Stop worrying." In a louder voice for Frank to hear, she added, "Have a drink but be careful. I think Frank may have perfected drinking to an art form."

Frank pretended to be offended. "'Tis a curse, so it is, but someone has to entertain our new arrivals," he nodded at Lily, "and welcome our Irishmen coming home."

Lily laughed at Frank's antics before letting herself into the house. Nobody locked their doors in this town, something else that was different and took a while to get used to.

"Is that yourself, Mrs. Doherty?" A voice called from the kitchen direction as Maeve made her way. "Would ye like some tea? Oh, you are on your own. I can have it ready in two minutes. Would you like to sit in the dining room?"

"Would you join me, Mrs. O'Reilly?"

"Call me Maeve, dear. I'd love that. If you don't mind, would it suit you to have it in the kitchen so I can keep an eye on the dinner?"

Lily took off her hat, gloves, and coat. "I'll just put these upstairs and be down in a bit. Please call me Lily, I still expect to see Carmel, Charlie's grandmother, when people say Mrs. Doherty."

Lily pushed the door to the kitchen area open, her mouth watering at the smell of the food bubbling on the stove. Maeve turned as the door creaked, a smile of welcome on her face, yet her eyes showed a hint of embarrassment.

"You have a lovely home, Mrs. I mean, Maeve." Lily tried to put the woman at ease.

"Sure, it's nothing like what you live in, but it is grand for my purposes."

Lily smiled as she took the seat the woman indicated. "I think you'd be surprised at the places I've lived in."

Maeve's eyes widened with curiosity.

"When I met Charlie, I was working for a doctor, looking after her daughter." Lily didn't see the need to elaborate on what her working life had been before she met Doc Erin. There was little point in raking over her past, especially as it was certain to make Maeve uncomfortable.

"A female doctor. Well, I never."

Lily grinned. "Doc Erin is a very special lady. Carmel Doherty used to work as her housekeeper; that's how we all got to know one another. Doc Erin was visiting New York when an awful blizzard came, and we all had to pull together to get through the storm. Charlie saved a man's life, and he was gracious enough to help him get a new job. He studied hard and became an attorney."

"A solicitor. And you, his wife, sitting in my kitchen. Are you sure you wouldn't rather sit upstairs in the dining room?"

"No, this suits me just fine." Lily glanced around the cozy room, noting the dresser stacked with dishes on one side of the wall, the well-scrubbed table they were sitting at, the blackened stove. Cook would be very impressed by this clean kitchen. "It's very homely."

"Aye. I have a young girl who comes in to clean and do some other chores. Now that I'm getting on in years, I can't do everything. And it helps her out too; the family have need of her earnings. There are many families around hereabouts that don't have full stomachs going to bed of an evening."

"That's the same in New York. We try to help, but..." Lily didn't continue. What was the point? They did a little, but it was never enough.

"I thought the streets of America were paved with gold," the woman smiled to show she was teasing, but her face held a curious expression.

"For some, they are. For most, it's the same as everywhere else. A struggle to survive from one day to the next. There are so many immigrants into New York now; there is huge competition for jobs, and people take advantage of that."

"'Tis the same everywhere. The rich get richer, and the poor..."

Maeve reached over and patted Lily on the

hand before giving the contents of the teapot a big stir. Then she poured out the tea, and they chatted about this and that.

"Frank says he will drive us down to see where Carmel and Joseph grew up. He thinks some of Charlie's cousins may still live nearby."

"Sure, the whole of Ireland is related," Maeve finished her tea. "Will you have another one?"

Lily shook her head. Maeve picked up Lily's cup, looking into the bottom of it. Her actions reminded Lily of Granny Belbin. A chill ran down her back despite her protests to Kathleen that reading tea leaves was a load of nonsense.

"Do you want me to read your fortune, Lily?"

"No, but thank you."

Maeve held her gaze before she laughed. "I'm teasing you, love. I wouldn't have a notion where to start. 'Tis not a gift I was blessed with."

Lily couldn't stop the sigh of relief escaping.

Maeve reached over and took Lily's hand. "I don't need the tea leaves to see that you carry a heavy burden. My mother always told me a sorrow shared was one halved. Not sure I agree with that, not fully at any rate, but I'm a good listener if you want to talk. I'm not a gossip either. What you tell me will stay between you, me, and these tea leaves." Maeve smiled, but her eyes held such a look of understanding Lily thought for a second the woman could read minds. Despite having only met Maeve the night before, she found herself telling her everything.

"There was a fire in New York before we came here. A factory. Almost 150 women lost their lives, others, including a friend, were terribly injured. I just can't shake the idea that it was partly my fault."

"Did you own this factory?"

Lily shook her head.

"Work in it?"

"No."

Maeve tilted her head to one side. "Not sure I understand. You didn't set the fire, did you?"

"Of course not."

"So explain how you could be responsible? 'Cause I'm lost, love."

"The women who worked there went out on strike about a year before the fire. I supported them, but I could have done more. I knew the conditions in the factories were dangerous. I should have done something."

"Like what?"

"I don't know, but something. After the strikes and another fire, not in New York, I decided to open my own factory. We already employ some women as seamstresses. I persuaded some wealthy friends to buy some land and build it, but the work took too long. The factory only opened last month, and that fire was last April."

"Oh, my dear, none of that is your fault. Was the factory where those unfortunate women died the only unsafe workplace in New York? No, of course, it wasn't. You are only one woman and, while you seem capable enough, you are not in charge of the city. You don't make the rules."

"My head knows all that, but I just feel so, so tired. Of everything. I want to curl up in a corner and watch the world go by. Just for a bit."

"You are a mother of five, you told me. What age did you start working?"

"When I was thirteen, or thereabouts." Lily

didn't want to face that part of her past. That hurt was old news.

"So, you have been working for about thirty years, give or take. You are a wife and a mother, and you have this business that employs seamstresses. Do you do anything else?"

"A bit. I help organize orphan trains – they take the poorer orphans off the streets of New York and get them new families. Well, that's the idea, but in reality, it wasn't working too well."

"So you jumped in to fix that too?"

Lily played with the cup on the table. She didn't like the way that sounded but wasn't about to offend the older woman either.

"I don't mean you are a busybody, Lily. To me, you seem to be a very caring woman who has taken too much on herself and is now paying the price. You are exhausted and grieving for those people who died and the families left behind. For the children who don't find good homes and the ones you can't save. Sounds to me like you have spent years looking after everyone else and very little time on yourself. I know that's the way the world works, but nothing comes free. Caring for others takes its toll just as surely as working in the fields all his life has Frank's back stooped. So, what made you come to Ireland? Did you run away?"

Lily looked up. "I didn't want to come," she whispered. "Charlie has been talking about coming 'home' for years. But it was never the right time. First, he was helping me with 'Carmel's Mission' and building up his own practice. Then we had the children, and the years just went past. But the fire affected him too. Not so much at the time, although of course he cared about the people. It was the trial. When the men who owned the factory were found innocent, his belief in everything just died. He passionately believed in our justice system, and now he doesn't. He said he wanted to come to Ireland and a good friend of ours, Kathleen, told me it was time to support my husband, to put him first. It wasn't the right time. There is so much to do with the new factory and everything. But... here I am."

"How well does this friend know you?"

Lily thought of Kathleen and all they had shared over the last almost twenty years. "Better than anyone."

"Perhaps she knew how much you needed a break but also knew telling you that wouldn't work, so she used your love for your husband instead." Maeve smiled so gently, Lily's eyes filled with tears.

"Let them fall, Lily. A good cry never hurt anyone. You have a huge heart but you have to take time to look after yourself. You can't help anyone if you are broken inside. Your friend Kathleen knew you needed a holiday. Charlie loves you, you can see that from the way he looks at you. Try to enjoy your time together and then when you get back to New York, you can take up the reins of saving the world once more." Maeve winked as she said this last sentence.

"Thank you, Maeve. You are a very wise woman."

"Well I'm old and they say experience comes with a long life. Not sure about the wise bit but thank you, dear. Now why don't you take yourself off for a long nap. Sleep is a great cure too."

## CHAPTER 12

*T*he next morning they walked out the door expecting to see the man from the station.

"Young Flinty got a job, so he asked me to take you out to visit the old place instead," Frank said as he pulled up outside the guesthouse. His horse, a beautiful docile black mare, nudged Lily's shoulder as if expecting an apple or other treat.

Lily rubbed the mare's nose. "I'm sorry, I don't have anything for you, beautiful." The horse snorted but nudged her again.

"She likes you. A good judge of character, she is. Let's be off before those rain clouds roll over and drown us."

They headed out of town, going in the opposite direction from where they had gone to see the sea, now headed inland.

"Frank, what's that statue of the woman?" Lily admired the 16-foot marble statue of a woman standing on what looked like broken chains, holding a flag at half-mast.

Frank eased through the traffic, pulling to a stop so Lily could get a better look. "That's the Lady Erin Monument. They put it up in 1899 to commemorate the anniversary of the 1798 rebellion," he explained, glancing around before continuing. "The lady represents Ireland, standing on the broken chains, symbolizing our struggle for freedom from the English."

Lily gaped at the statue. "I thought Ireland was still part of the British Empire."

Frank spat. "Ireland has never been part of any empire, British or otherwise. We are our own country, and the sooner they realize that, the better." He tapped the horse and set off once more, leaving Lily to exchange a bemused glance with Charlie.

After traveling in silence for some time, Lily

apologized. "I'm sorry, Frank. I didn't mean to insult you."

"You didn't. I just hate that they put up the statue, and we still haven't got our freedom. Those English have a lot to answer for. They sit in their cozy government seats and decide what happens here. Some landowners have never even set foot in Ireland. They stole the land from our ancestors and don't care about the people living on it. Did you know thirty thousand people were forced to leave Ireland from just Sligo port alone? Thousands more left from Galway, Cork, Dublin, and Belfast. Over a million people gone, never to return. They were the lucky ones. About the same number died of brutal starvation, reduced to eating grass or turf at the end, the poor creatures. There was plenty of food in the country; nobody needed to starve. They continued to export grain and meat from Ireland to England during those years and every year since. We've had other famines, none as bad as back then, but look around you. The Irish people live in poverty. It's wrong, so it is. But maybe things will change. Maybe we will get Home Rule, and that will be the first step on our way to freedom. Commemorating those who died in the 1798 rebellion is all well and good, but it would be more fitting if we had achieved freedom first."

Lily and Charlie stayed silent, sensing the man just needed to vent.

About an hour passed before Frank pulled the horse to a stop. "We're here. Be careful getting down, watch where you walk, Lily. Wouldn't want to get that lovely dress covered in cow muck."

As THEY WALKED across the green field, Lily saw the remains of a dwelling up ahead. The stone walls, once sturdy and secure were now succumbing to the relentless advances of ivy and moss, the green tendrils winding through the crevices. All that remained of the roof were a few wooden beams, and there was no doorway as one side of the cottage seemed to have pushed into the other, stones from the walls strewn over the ground. Lily held her breath, despite not being from Ireland, the sadness seeping from the walls of the broken down cottage caught her in the back of the throat. She wrapped her arms around her chest as if to protect her from the misery, glancing at her husband. Charlie swiped a hand across his eyes as he stared at the dwelling. If you could call it that.

Frank coughed. "This was your great grandfather's house, Cormac Curran. He was evicted in September 1847. Nobody has lived here since."

The land agent," Frank spat at the name, "He was the one who did the Landlords dirty work. If a man fell behind on his rent, which of course with the loss of the potato crop and no work to be found, most landlords used it as an excuse to clear their land. He'd put the family out on the side of the road and to make sure they didn't return, he'd order the soldiers to tear the roof off the house and knock the side walls down. Course, if the family refused to leave, they just pulled the roof down on top of them."

Lily didn't want to hear anymore but she couldn't be rude and turn away.

"Nobody could help them either. They couldn't risk it see? If the landlord or that bas....my apologies Missus, that tyke of an agent heard of a family sheltering one that had been evicted, they – the soldiers would come back and destroy that house too. Didn't matter none if the family were siblings or father and son. They didn't have a heart."

There was no door but a gaping hole allowed them to see inside. A broken stool lay overturned by the fireplace choked with ashes. A clay pot and fragments of other dishes were scattered across the floor. Weeds sprouted through cracks in the floor, the interior walls or what was left of them covered in moss. On the one remaining wall, a wooden cross hung from a nail, a reminder that once upon a time a family had lived and laughed in this house.

"NINETEEN FAMILIES WERE evicted by the same landlord. A local man, by the name of Duffy took the job as land agent. He had the soul of a devil that one, turning his back on his own people."

Lily's ears pricked up at the mention of the name Duffy. Was Frank talking about Ned Duffy's father or grandfather? Carmel Doherty had stood up to the Duffys in New York, thwarting them at every turn. She shivered, thinking of how close Ned Duffy had come to destroying Charlie's sister, Nora, just like he had ruined the lives of many other innocent young women. Her eyes met those of her husband, and they exchanged a look of understanding. She knew he was recalling the circumstances of how they had met.

Frank spat on the ground before continuing his story. "The local priest tried to plead their case, but it fell on deaf ears. Those were bad years." He turned to Charlie, his eyes glistening. "Your great-grandfather, Carmel's daddy, he was here that day. He fought back and paid the price. He was never a man to back down. It destroyed him to watch his children starving."

"How did my grandmother get away? I mean, how did she survive after being thrown from her home and land?" Charlie asked.

"Joseph's family took her and her sister into their home, despite the penalties if they were caught. Joseph's father went to his landlord over at Lissadell House, a man named Sir Robert Gore-Booth, and told him that Joseph and Carmel were courting and wanted to wed. He asked him to pay for their passage to America. Sir Robert and his wife were good people. They didn't stay in their big house while the people were starving; they came out and gave out free food and help where they could, including buying coffins to bury the dead. Most of the dead were buried in mass graves, but Sir Robert gave dignity to those who had died. He even caught the famine fever. Maybe that's why his granddaughter is the way she is, her being so committed to the Irish cause," Frank said, shrugging, his voice rough with emotion.

Lily walked to her husband, taking his hands and squeezing them. Frank looked past them, out over the fields. "Cormac Curran was a fine man. I didn't know him well, but my father never had a bad word to say about him. Nobody did. The Duffys had to leave Ireland soon after; they knew if they stayed here, we'd get our revenge. They used their ill-gotten gains to pay for passage to New York, and that was the last we heard of them. I hope they had the luck of the devil over there and died young with no one to grieve them," Frank spat again. "I'll leave you for a bit. I'll wait over with the horse and cart."

Frank slowly strolled away, his back even more stooped. Lily put her arm around Charlie. "I'm sorry about your family. No wonder Carmel didn't want to talk about what had happened with her and the Duffys back in Ireland. I can understand why Ned Duffy's father steered clear of her. He probably didn't want the Irish community knowing what he and his family had done."

They stood in silence, contemplating the sad scene stretched out in front of them. Remembering how Carmel Doherty had stood up to the priest after the deaths during the blizzard, her protective instinct towards her family fully evident, Lily admired the woman even more. To lose her father and home in such tragic circumstances and then be forced to leave the country she loved would have destroyed most women, but not her husband's grandmother.

"I know I didn't know these people, but I feel them around me. It's like their spirits are still here. I know that doesn't make sense," Charlie whispered.

"I feel it too. So much sadness. Are you ready to say goodbye?" Lily watched her husband's face, concerned about the effect this visit was having on him. He looked at the pile of bricks once more, then nodded. "Despite seeing this, I'm glad I came here, and you are by my side. This is such a beautiful country. I know why my grandmother is so proud to be Irish."

As they made their way back to the horse and cart, they found Frank deep in discussion with a solidly built man in his mid to late forties. His clean-shaven face was etched with lines, not just the creases of middle age but those earned from working outdoors in the biting wind of Irish winters. His hair, once raven black, was now streaked with grey, particularly at the temples. Lily glanced from the man to her husband and back. Although Charlie was less weathered-looking, having spent the last twenty years of his life working indoors, there was more than a passing resemblance between the two men. Charlie tensed by her side, obviously noticing the resemblance as well.

The men stopped talking as Lily and Charlie drew closer. The stranger's eyes, deep blue almost violet, were sharp and observant.

His smile, as he wiped his hands on his coat and stepped forward, lit up his face. He held out his hand in greeting to Charlie. "Tom Doherty is the name. From what Frank tells me, we are family." His hands, calloused from years of working the land, had a gentle grip when he shook hands with Lily and then returned his attention back to Charlie. "My grandfather was brother to Joseph Doherty. I never met Joseph, but I heard plenty of stories about him and his wife. Her father, Cormac Curran, was a bit of a legend around these parts."

Tom put his arm around Charlie's shoulders. "Welcome home." He clapped Charlie soundly on the back. "Will you come home to meet the wife? Niamh would be delighted to have another woman to pass the time of day with." Tom smiled in Lily's direction. "My home might not be what you are used to, Mrs. Doherty, but the welcome and the fire will be warm."

"We'd love to, Mr. Doherty, but perhaps you should check with your wife if it is convenient," Lily replied.

Tom and Frank burst out laughing at Lily's

words. "Call me Tom. We don't stand on ceremony around here. A man, or woman, is always welcome. A door is never closed to guests. Frank knows the way; he'll drive you. Unless you'd like to walk with me. These lands once belonged to our ancestors." The invitation was directed to Charlie, who looked torn between accompanying Lily and going with his newfound cousin.

"I'll be fine with Frank. You go ahead."

"You'd be welcome too, Mrs. Doherty, but those boots would get ruined, and it's a bit of a way to the house."

Despite the kind invitation, Lily sensed the man wanted some time alone with her husband. "Please call me Lily. I will ride with Frank and meet you there later."

Charlie helped Lily into the cart and Frank drove her off down the road leaving the two men looking after them. "It was nice of you to arrange for Tom to be here to meet Charlie."

"I'd love to claim the credit, but it was a coincidence. He was down checking his fields; a couple of his sheep have wandered off. He saw us and recognized me."

They drove on in silence, the road meandering around corners with green fields for miles either side of them. The rain held off and the sun, although not warm, was pleasant. She was glad of her thick coat and gloves as the wind was chilly.

LILY SAW A MODEST, whitewashed farmhouse situated on the side of a hill, smoke billowing out from a chimney in the center of the thatched roof, into the blue, cloudless sky. A couple of outbuildings, also made from stone, were set back from the house. From the noises coming from them, she assumed that was where the animals were kept. Frank got down to open the gate leading into the property before he led the horse up the road.

A little girl ran out of the house, her curls the color of polished mahogany, her blue eyes opening wide as she took in the visitors. "Mammy, Mammy, there's a woman out here. She looks like they do from the big house."

"What are you talking about, Deirdre? There's no... oh my goodness." The slender woman with chestnut hair pulled back into a bun, a couple of strands escaping to frame a face dotted with freckles. Curiosity and a little fear mixed in her eyes as she pulled the child to her side. The door of the dwelling behind her opened, and a young boy carrying a piglet walked out.

"Mammy, the old sow keeps kicking this... oh."

Lily saw the boy was the image of his father. He had the same sturdy frame, his jet-black hair, and blue-violet eyes that sparkled with more than a hint of mischief. He openly stared at her before the squeaking of the piglet reminded him to let the animal down. Once he did, the piglet ran off.

"Peter Doherty, you better catch him before your dad gets home."

With a gulp, the boy ran off in search of the animal. Deirdre remained at her mother's side, her hand clutching the woman's skirt.

"Niamh, this is Mrs. Lily Doherty, recently arrived from America. Her husband, Charlie, is a cousin of your Tom. Tom invited us to come for tea."

Niamh took a step forward, wiping her hand on her skirt as Frank helped Lily down from the cab.

"Nice to meet you." Niamh smiled, but her smile didn't reach her green eyes. She turned her head to look at her home and then back at Lily. "Come in, please. Deirdre, go fetch me some water for the tea."

"Yes, Mammy." Deirdre gave Lily a shy smile before she took off running.

"Come in and make yourself at home." Niamh led the way into the house. Frank stood back to allow Lily to walk into the house first. She saw the kitchen garden enclosed by a wooden fence. Someone had been busy getting it ready for planting. Inside the house, it was simply furnished, with a large hearth being the centerpiece of the main living area. Judging by the cooking pot hanging over it, the fire was both a source of heat and a place to cook. The stone floor would have been cold but for the handmade woven rugs strewn about. The windows were small, covered by thick curtains likely needed to keep the cold out. There was a table with four chairs on one side of the room, with what looked like a settle bed on the other. Someone had fixed a couple of cabinets to the wall above the table. A small dresser held a few plates, cups, and saucers. The house was clean, but she sensed her new family didn't have much to spare.

"Please take a seat. Will you have a cup of tea? Or a glass of milk or water?" Niamh put some more peat on the fire.

"Tea would be lovely, thank you. I'm sorry to just turn up like this. I thought your husband and mine would be here already."

Frank coughed, clearing his throat noisily. "They likely got to talking. Tom may have taken Charlie to the local pub. That's not a bad idea. If you ladies don't mind, I shall go and have a look for them."

Frank was gone before Lily could protest. She glanced helplessly at the other woman and saw the same look of discomfort on her face. Deirdre arrived back with a small bucket of water. Lily moved to relieve her of her burden, but Niamh got there first. "Take a seat, Mrs. Doherty. I'll just boil the water."

"Please, call me Lily. Deirdre is a lovely name for a beautiful girl." Deirdre looked at her shyly. She put a hand out to touch Lily but her mother's bark stopped her.

"Don't, you'll get her coat dirty. Haven't you

chores to do? The eggs won't jump into the basket themselves."

"Yes, Mammy." The child flashed a quick smile at Lily before running out again, her bare feet tapping across the floor.

"She's adorable." Lily wasn't sure if she should take her coat off or not. She stood by the chair, hesitating, wishing she had insisted that Tom arrange a visit rather than springing the surprise.

"Go on, take a seat. Oh, do you want to take your coat off? I could hang it up over here." Niamh held out her hand to take the coat. When Lily handed it to her, Niamh touched the fabric almost in awe.

"It was a Christmas present. Our friends got married on New Year's Eve and Charlie insisted I have a new coat. He picked it out himself." Lily babbled, taking her seat at the table.

"'Tis beautiful. I just hope it doesn't get dirty on you."

"It will be fine. I'm sorry that I just appeared. I didn't mean to interrupt your day, but your husband insisted."

"Ah, that's men for you. I've nothing to give

you but a slice of brown bread and some jam we made from the blackberries we collected last autumn. Would you like that?"

"A cup of tea would be perfect, thank you. You live in a gorgeous place, the views are incredible. Ireland is such a pretty place. Not a bit like where I live."

"You're a city lady?" Niamh set the cup and saucer in front of Lily with a jug of milk. She placed the teapot on a crocheted doily before taking a seat herself. She stirred the contents of the pot and then poured it for them.

"We live in New York. We have a few pretty parks nearby, Central Park being the largest, but it's not like living here."

Niamh glanced at Lily's now ungloved hands and then at her own, possibly comparing the white, soft skin with her own cracked, red hands.

"It must be challenging work, raising children and doing farm work, especially when it rains so much." Lily smiled. "Before I met Charlie, I lived out west, in Colorado. We had to go to the well for water and there was a lot of scrubbing trying to keep the floors and all free of the dust and muck. It didn't rain much, not compared to here. But when it did, the streets turned to mud. Then in the summer, with the sun being so strong, the dust was fierce. Between the horses and cattle, the streets were never clean, and you can just imagine how hard we women worked."

At last, Niamh smiled, her eyes dancing with amusement. "'Tis the same everywhere. The men think they have it hard, but us women could teach them a thing or two about work." Niamh took a sip of her tea. "Is Colorado far from New York? Is that where you met your husband? Is he a cowboy?"

"Charlie? No, not at all. He worked on the trains, and we met in New York."

They heard laughing outside. Niamh stood up. "I should see what the children are up to."

"I'll come with you, if that's alright."

Niamh eyed her clothes. "You should stay here. The pigsty is no place for that dress. I'll be back in a minute."

*Charlie, hurry up.* Lily took another drink of tea. Where was her husband, and how much longer would she have to make small talk with this stranger? She could see Niamh wasn't being rude; she seemed to be naturally shy and obviously ill at ease. Niamh's clothes were clean but obviously well-worn. Lily wondered how many more children there were. Peter and Deirdre were clean and well looked after, but their clothes were patched.

When Niamh returned, the children came with her. They pulled out stools and sat at the table, both of them staring at her. "Are you really from America?" Peter asked.

"Yes. Charlie, my husband, and I sailed from New York to Southampton, and then we got a boat from Liverpool to Dublin."

"Wow. Imagine seeing all those places. We've never left Sligo."

"You're very young. When you're older, I'm sure you will see places too."

"Mammy, did you ever see England?"

"No. I've no interest in ever visiting that place. Now, shush and have your tea."

Peter took a sip but he hadn't finished with the questions. "What was the ship like? Was it big?"

"Very. It has to be to cross the ocean."

"Were you scared? I would be. All that water." Deirdre shuddered.

"Girls." Peter rolled his eyes, earning him a light belt with the tea towel.

"Mind your manners, son. We don't want this fine lady to think we are heathens."

"What's a heathen?" Peter responded, but at a look from his mother, he turned red before picking up his cup again.

"I was a little frightened. It was my first time on a ship. But Charlie had been wanting to come to Ireland for years. His grandparents came from Sligo, and he wanted to see where they had been born and lived. Some friends of ours got married and moved to London, so we traveled with them. London is a nice city, but I prefer the countryside. You live in a beautiful place. It's so green."

"That's all the rain. Daddy says it makes everything grow." Deirdre spoke up. "I like your dress; you have very pretty hair, too. And your ears sparkle."

Lily touched her ear; she had forgotten she was wearing the earrings Mr. Prentice had given her when she got married.

"They were a gift from a special friend when I married Charlie. Would you like to try them on?"

Deirdre's eyes went as wide as saucers. "Can I? Mammy?"

"I don't think so," Niamh shook her head.

"Please." Both Lily and Deirdre spoke at the same time. "I don't mind, Niamh. They clip on and off like this." Lily took one off and showed them how the clasp worked. "May I?" she asked Niamh, who nodded. She took the second earring off and put them on Deirdre's ears.

"Can I look in your mirror, Mammy? It's a special occasion; I won't break it."

Niamh pushed the chair back and, reaching up for a box on top of the cabinet, took it down, opening it to remove a silver hairbrush and mirror set.

"That's beautiful."

"It was my mother's. It was passed down to me when she died."

She held the mirror up to Deirdre, who turned her head this way and that, laughing at herself. "Look at my ears, Mammy; they're like candles from the church the way they sparkle. They're so pretty." Deirdre carefully took them off before handing them to her mom. "Why don't you try them on? I think you'll be even more beautiful than you are. Miss Lily won't mind, will you?"

Lily shook her head. Niamh hesitated.

"Please try them if you'd like to."

Niamh put them on and looked at her reflection in wonder.

"You should ask Daddy to buy you a pair when he's next at the big market." Deirdre's innocent remark caused Niamh to almost tear the earrings from her ears. She handed them back to Lily before repacking the mirror and brush into its case and returning it to their special place.

"I've no need for fancy trinkets, Deirdre. Don't be putting ideas in your daddy's head when he comes back, you hear me?"

"Yes, Mammy, sorry Mammy."

Lily took the ear bobs and put them back on. She glanced at her watch before standing up.

"It's time to leave you to your day. If you could point me in the direction of the town.."

Niamh blushed. "Please don't go. I didn't mean to snap at the child. Will you have another cup of tea?"

Lily shook her head. She couldn't drink another one, she'd drown.

"It wasn't fair of me just to turn up unannounced. You and your beautiful children have been lovely company but it's time I was going. If I knew how to get back to Sligo town, I would head there but I imagine it would take an hour or so to walk and I might get lost."

"If you're set on going, we'll walk you down to the town."

Uncomfortable about dragging Niamh away from her work, Lily knew she had no choice. It wasn't like New York where she could hail a cab or jump on a bus.

"Thank you." Lily put on her coat and hat as Niamh banked down the fire, got Deirdre ready and then put a red shawl around her own shoulders.

"What about your son?"

"He'll be grand here with the animals. He has no time for town."

Lily didn't think this was wise, but it wasn't her place to say anything. She headed out the door of the cottage waiting for Niamh to follow her and lock up. Instead, the woman just closed over the door.

"Are you not afraid of someone robbing you?"

Niamh looked genuinely confused. "Who would rob us? Nobody around here would touch our things unless there was good reason. Then they'd replace what they took. Is it not like that over in America?"

Lily was about to say no but stopped. "Not where I live in New York but I'm sure there are areas like it. Clover Springs in Colorado where Carmel Doherty now lives and areas like that. The city life is different."

"It is that."

Niamh walked along side her in companionable silence with Deirdre skipping ahead of them.

## CHAPTER 13

*K*athleen walked out to the kitchen where the children had gathered to enjoy some warm cookies just out of the oven.

"Max, Nettie, when you have finished, can you come to my office, please. I want to talk to you both."

Max glanced at his sister who shoved the rest of her cookie in her mouth and stood up.

"We're ready now."

The children followed her to the office and sat down, Nettie almost sitting on her brother.

Kathleen smiled, "I have a very special letter I want to read to you."

"From who?" Max asked eyeing the envelope suspiciously. Nettie settled close to Max, her thumb in her mouth.

"A lady and gentleman who wish to give you both a home. My sister Bridget met them and gave them the address to write to you. Will I read it?"

Max shrugged but his arm went around Nettie's shoulders as she moved closer to his side.

*"Dear Max and Nettie*

*WE WISH we could come to New York to meet you but we cant leave our farm. Mrs Watson,"*

KATHLEEN LOOKED up from the letter to explain. "That's Bridget ,my sister's married name". The children just stared at her so she continued reading.

*"Mrs. Watson has told us all about you both. She said you needed a home and you would like to live together. We would love that. We don't have any children, not anymore. We had twin boys, but they died young from the fever. We have a nice house, not very big but it has a large bedroom that we can*

split into two to give you a room each. We have a small farm with a few pigs, some sheep and a milk cow. We don't want to offer you a home so that you work for us. We want you to be part of our family. We would like you to go to school. Mrs Collins is an excellent teacher. Most of the local children go to school so you should make lots of friends. Mrs Watson says some of the children you already know are coming to live at the orphanage. They would go to school too so you can still see them.

WE LIVE a little way outside of town but Elmer will take you to school and collect you the first few days until you know the way. Then you can walk — somedays I will be able to drive you if Elmer isn't using the wagon.

WE DON'T HAVE MUCH in the way of money but we have plenty of love to give to you should you want to come and live with us. We have enclosed a photograph we had taken on our wedding day. It was some years back but we never got the opportunity to have another one taken.

. . .

*PLEASE WRITE BACK and let us know if you would like to come and make a family with us. If you want to call us Aunt and Uncle, that will be fine. We don't want to replace your dear mother, please don't think that. We are not looking to replace our boys. But we thought seeing as we understand the pain of loss and you do too, the four of us might make a new family remembering our twins and your mother all the time.*

*PLEASE WRITE and let us know what you think,*

*YOURS sincerely*

*ELMER AND PEARL HAVERFORD.*

KATHLEEN COUGHED after reading the letter, overwhelmed by the warmth and under-standing Mrs. Haverford had shown assuming she had written it. Too many people didn't think of how the sudden tragic death of a parent would affect such young children. She looked up from the letter to see Max staring at it.

"Would you like to read it for yourself?"

Max nodded.

Kathleen handed him the letter and excused herself. "I'll just go check with Cook about something. I will be back in a few minutes. You take your time reading the letter and discussing what you would like to say in a letter back.

"Do we have to go to these people?"

"No Max. Nobody will force you to go to live with the Haverfords but so far they are the only suitable family to offer both you and Nettie a place together. Everyone else has offered to take one child only."

# CHAPTER 14

*L*ily sat at the table in the Doherty household, Frank having dropped her off before taking Charlie into town for what he called a bit of business.

She watched Niamh make lace.

"You have such a delicate touch. That piece is really beautiful."

Niamh blushed a little but Lily thought she was pleased. It was hard to tell as the woman hadn't been in good humour all morning. She'd been crying when Lily had walked in although she tried to pretend everything was fine. Lily had seen her shove a brown envelope under the box that contained the hairbrush.

Niamh had welcomed her but her welcome

169

lacked the warmth she'd displayed in the last week they'd gotten to know one another. Lily couldn't help but worry but she didn't feel she could ask what was wrong. Especially not in front of Niamh's family.

"Does everyone dress like you in New York? Your skirt is much shorter than the ladies wear around here," Louise, Niamh's daughter who was on a day off, asked, her hands hovering but not quite touching Lily's dress.

"Louise, keep your hands and comments to yourself. You'll only make her dirty."

"She's fine. I have a daughter of a similar age at home. Evie, she's just turned fourteen."

Louise blushed. "I'll be fourteen on my next birthday. What's she like? Does she wear dresses like you?"

"Evie loves to go shopping. She has an eye for color, knows by looking at someone what would suit them. She wants to own a dress shop."

Louise sat at the table, her head sitting on her hands as she stared at Lily. "Do you have any other children?"

"Four more. Twin boys who are like chalk and cheese. Teddy and Laurie. Laurie is mad about flying and airplanes. My daughter, Grace, she's sixteen, always has her head in a book, she wants to be a teacher. She's always had a gift for languages. She speaks German and Yiddish and a little bit of French." Lily smiled thinking of her bookish daughter. "Coleen, she'll be nine in the Summer. She wants to be a nurse or at least that is what she wanted to do the week before we left. It changes depending on her mood. What about you, Louise, what would you like to do?"

The girl turned scarlet. "I'd like to be a teacher too, but I work as a maid in the big house…"

Niamh swiped her daughter across the head with a tea cloth. "Don't be telling Lily about your silly notions, girl. People like us, they don't become teachers. Louise is lucky; she's secured a position in the big house. She started last September."

Lily didn't want to be rude, but she couldn't help but feel sorry for Louise. Clearly, she was a bright young woman and probably found working as a maid boring.

"Don't pay any mind to that one. She's always dreaming. Been like that since she was a child, and my aul mam told her tales of all the neighbors who left for America." Niamh frowned. "I don't mean to be forward, but it's not like many of them had the luck of the Dohertys. Most are just getting by if that. It's a few of them that can afford to come back and see those they left behind."

Lost for words, Lily kept silent. Had the contents of the envelope lead to Niamh's short temper.

She was glad when her husband chose that moment to pop his head through the top half of the door, a large box in his arms.

"There you are, I thought you'd run off with a local." She teased him, trying to lighten the mood.

He laughed. "I might have been tempted but Tom kept me in check. Turning to Niamh he asked, "Will I just leave this on the table?"

"What have you got there, Charlie? We don't need none of your charity."

"Aw will you leave the boy be. It's not charity when it's family. Give us the baccy for my pipe?" Tom held his hand out.

"Niamh, this." Charlie pointed at the box, "is only a small thank you for putting up with us and showing us such wonderful hospitality."

Niamh stared at him open-mouthed before she unpacked the contents. A bottle of whiskey, a couple of bottles of stout, a tin of tea, packets of sugar, flour, salt, and other staples soon covered the kitchen table. The children gasped when they saw the candy.

"Can we have some sweets, Mam? Please?" Deirdre begged, reminding Lily that's what they called candy in Ireland.

"Sure, go on, you might as well. Your cousin has deep pockets."

"Niamh Doherty, that's enough."

Niamh turned scarlet at her husband's reprimand. Putting her hands to her face, she muttered something as she ran out of the door of the cottage.

"Tom, I'm sorry. I didn't mean to…"

"Don't you be apologizing, lad. She's a good woman is my Niamh, but times are hard and… well, I won't be ruining your holiday with our tales of woe. Would you like a smoke?"

Charlie shook his head. Lily put a hand on his arm before she turned and followed Niamh out of the house. She looked around the small farmholding, wondering where the woman had gone before she spotted her walking toward the wood. Gathering up her skirts, Lily moved as fast as she could, eventually catching up with Niamh. The woman was sitting by the stream, oblivious to the wet grass soaking her skirt as she sobbed her heart out. Lily hesitated, unsure of whether to comfort or turn back before the woman saw her. At that moment, Niamh glanced behind her, spotting Lily.

"Niamh, we're sorry. We didn't mean to cause trouble between you and Tom or offense. You have been so good to us. We just wanted to do something small."

"Small is it? When you produce enough food to keep my family for the next month!"

Lily took a step back from the bitterness in both her tone and face.

"I'm sorry. I best leave you to it." Lily turned to go but stopped as the woman's sobs grew louder.

"Niamh, what is it? Can I help?"

Niamh shook her head but Lily moved to her side anyway. She took a seat on a nearby stone, not wanting to sit in the wet grass.

"A problem shared and all that. It may help to talk to a stranger."

"You're a lady. You wouldn't know what it's like, not being able to keep your children fed and clothed; to let them have their dreams."

Lily took the other woman's hands in hers. "Appearances can be deceptive. I was once poorer than you. I didn't have a roof over my head." At the look of disbelief on Niamh's face, Lily nodded, "We are comfortable now, but it wasn't always that way. Charlie rescued a man back in the blizzards of 1888, and that man helped him in more ways than we can count. I was lucky too, I met a lovely lady called Doc Erin, she knew Charlie's grandmother. That's how we met. Things were hard to start with, but they got easier because we let others help us. Just talk to me. I promise I won't tell Charlie, not if you don't want me to."

Niamh rubbed her eyes on her sleeve. "I'm grateful to you and Charlie. I should be ashamed of myself for what I said, how I acted. It's just so difficult. Louise is so unhappy. She doesn't moan about it, she knows we need the money, but I can see it in her. I can see it in her walk, her head almost touching her knees when she heads out the door of a morning after spending her one day off a month here with us. We kept her at school longer than most girls of her age. But when the job at the house came up, we had to grab it. We only got it because I used to work up there before I was married. The housekeeper liked me, knew I was a worker."

"I'm sure Louise will find her way." Lily tried to soothe the woman.

"She has her heart set on teaching, and she's good at it. She has the patience of a saint with the younger ones, answering all their questions, helping them do their figures and all. She could join the convent, plenty of the sisters are teachers, but that's not the right life for her. She has too much spirit for a start."

"Is there anything else bothering you?"

"Ah Lily, I don't know what to make of the world around me. It's so beautiful around here with the sound of the waves on the shore, the clean air, and green grass as far as the eye can see. But that's what the visitors like you see. To us, we see the land that is too weak or stone-filled to grow a good crop, cattle that can be decimated by disease, cows that stop giving milk, the hens that are stolen by foxes, the rents that are too high, the arrears that mount up when the crop fails." Niamh barely stopped to take a breath. Lily sensed things had been building for a while. She didn't move, just listened as the woman continued, "Then there are the boys. Ireland wants to be free, and I understand that. Heck, I even support it, but I don't want to lose my boys to the cause. My family paid a high enough price when my grandfather was transported to Australia."

Lily couldn't stop the shocked noise she made. She'd heard of Irish and some English people being sent to live in the colonies, but she had never met someone who was personally affected.

"Aye, the British sent him to Australia for being a Fenian. Said he was a would-be murderer. My grandpa wasn't going to kill anyone. They never found a gun or anything on him or when they searched the house. He stood up to the local landowner, a man by the name of Lord Walton, when he tried to increase rents again after the potato crop failed in 1867. The people could remember the real famine, and they were terrified it was going to happen again. People were panicking, and my grandfather and some other men told them not to pay their rents but to buy food for their families instead. My grandfather argued that the rents could be paid when the next harvest came in, the landowners being so wealthy they could afford to wait. Lord Walton was a magistrate, and he convicted my grandfather and two other men of treason and sent them to Botany Bay. My grandmother and her three children would have starved but for having wonderful neighbors. My mother went to work in the big house as a skivvy at the age of ten. I followed in her footsteps. I would have stayed there too but for meeting my Tom."

Lily didn't know what to say. She reached into her pocket and drew out a clean hanky, passing it to Niamh to dry her tears.

"And now my boys want to join the revolutionaries. Both Seamus and Declan are away above in Dublin, and you should hear the stuff they come out with when they come home to visit. They have both joined unions, and if their employer finds out, they will be out of jobs."

Lily sighed. So it was the same in Ireland as it was in the USA. She could see the women marching through the streets of New York, demanding fairer wages and better working conditions. That strike had lasted a long time, and many families had paid a high price.

"There have been lockouts and minor skirmishes throughout the last year, some of them led by women. Declan told me he admires some woman called Rosie Hackett who works at Jacobs Biscuit factory with him. She was out with the strikers last year before he joined. If they go out again, he says he won't be a scab. I don't want him to be. I agree they are fighting for better wages, but we need his money. And it's not like those in Dublin Castle need much of an excuse to lock up our Irish lads. Dear Lord, above, if not for the money the boys send us, we would have lost the farm months back. I suppose I should be counting my blessings; my boys still live in Ireland. I don't have to hold an American wake for them."

"What's an American wake?" Lily asked.

"Same as a wake for the dead only there is no body. Usually when people travel to America, they are never seen again in Ireland so the family gets together to mourn their passing." Niamh wiped her face with her apron. "I should be counting my blessings not behaving like a silly old woman. My boys are still in Ireland and I get to see them every few months."

Niamh stood up to head back to the cottage.

"If there is anything we can do to help, Niamh, please just say."

Niamh took her arm. "I'm sorry for being a wet blanket. Let's go back and see if the children left any sweets for us. Not that we should be eating them with it being lent and all but sure it's not every day your family comes visiting from America, is it?"

Lily didn't know what Lent was but she said nothing. Niamh was trying to put a smile on her face and she wasn't about to do anything to ruin that. She'd talk to Charlie later to see if there was anything they could do but for now, she let Niamh lead her back to the cottage.

CHAPTER 15

athleen glanced around the table, all their friends gathered together for a meal in the sanctuary dining room. Pascal Griffin sat next to Emily with Father Nelson on his other side. Gustav sat on the other side of his wife, with Leonie to his right. Richard sat between herself and Richard. Only Conrad and Maria were missing due to Maria not feeling too well.

Pascal sat back in the chair. "Cook really outdid herself this evening, Kathleen. I think I shall have to loosen my belt."

"I thought it was on its last notch already."

Pascal turned to the priest. "That's not very

charitable. Wait till I see your bishop; I shall make a formal complaint."

Father Nelson rolled his eyes. "If this Bishop heard anything but complaints about me, he wouldn't be happy. That man goes out of his way to find things he dislikes."

Kathleen hid a smile as Father Nelson blessed himself, probably asking forgiveness for making unkind remarks. Having met the Bishop, Kathleen believed the man had been born with a perpetual frown on his face. "Your Bishop would find something to complain about if he found himself alone on a deserted Island. Don't pay him any heed. He has no taste or else he is jealous as he knows we all love you."

Father Nelson waved away her praise, but she knew she'd made him feel better. The Bishop appeared to go out of his way to make life difficult for the poor man, and at his advanced years, he hadn't the energy he once had.

Kathleen stood up. "Shall we go into the fire? Ethel set up the tea tray and some cake in there if anyone is still hungry."

"I might be able to fit in a slice of cake." Pascal flashed a look at his wife.

She rolled her eyes. "So long as you don't complain to me tomorrow when your suit won't close."

Emily and Leonie exchanged a grin as the latter wheeled herself into the other room. Everyone followed, with Richard holding the door open for Kathleen to go ahead of him. Once they were seated, the conversation began again.

"Kathleen, why don't you go with the children to Riverside Springs? It's obvious you are worried about Bridget, and it will give you a chance to see Shane and Angel, not to mention meet your nieces and nephews. You can also catch up with Bella, Meg, and the other children you helped to rescue. I think it would do you the world of good."

Before Kathleen could say a word to Father Nelson, Richard cut in.

"I agree."

"I can't. Aside from my own children, I promised Lily I would mind her children and the sanctuary and then there's the factory."

Richard leaned in. "Why not take our children with you? Miss Cooper would help you. Grace Doherty is managing just fine without any input from us, and I'm here if she needs assistance."

Emily put her teacup back on its saucer. "I can call in and check on them as well, if that would put your mind at ease or I can move into Lily's house if you think that would help. Gustav can look after himself for a few days." She leaned forward. "I think it's a wonderful idea. The Chiver children are terrified of leaving Leonie here in New York, and having you on the train would help a lot to ease their fears. Then there is Max and Nettie. They have both formed a very strong attachment to you."

Although very tempted, Kathleen shook her head. "Thank you all, but I couldn't do it. Lily left me in charge. What would she say if I took off to visit Bridget."

Father Nelson leaned back in his chair, crossing his legs at his ankles. "I think she would be the first one to cheer you on. I know you are worried about Bridget's health. You haven't seen your siblings for years. Also, think about what you can do for the Orphan Train society."

Kathleen looked at him blankly.

"My dear Kathleen, the Orphan Train society doesn't believe we can send any more orphans to Riverside and surrounding areas. They favor sending the children further afield. Perhaps it is time we reminded them of the excellent work that has been achieved by the Watsons and people like them."

Kathleen burst out laughing at the serious look on Father Nelson's face, catching the twinkle in his eye. "You are making this up as you go along, aren't you Father? I think you and my husband have been colluding, perhaps with the help of our own dear Inspector." Kathleen gave Inspector Griffin a look; he colored in response.

"Leave me out of this although my life would be easier if you were to disappear for a week or so. I might not have to worry about handbag-wielding ladies attacking my police officers."

As Kathleen opened her mouth to defend herself, her friends laughed, making her laugh too.

"What do you think Leonie? You are very quiet."

"I think whatever you decide to do is the best choice."

"Don't be coy, Leonie. You must have an opinion."

Leonie looked at the floor as she became the center of attention, but then she took a deep breath and looked straight at Kathleen.

"If you could go, I would be very grateful. It's not that I don't trust the people organizing the orphan trains, but you hear lots of stories, and I want to make sure my siblings reach Riverside Springs. I don't want to break my promise to Mama that they will also stay together. I know I'm in this chair, but I can look after the sanctuary with Ethel and Cook if you trust me to do so."

Kathleen moved to Leonie's side, taking her hand. "Of course I trust you; we all do. I didn't think of asking you as you have so much work already. Richard says you are working very hard on your exercises, but they are very tiring. I don't want you withering away to nothing. I think Lily might kill me, and if she doesn't, I know a young man who might."

Leonie blushed at that. It wasn't a secret Kenny had written to her before he left New

York and promised to send letters from each of the ports his ship visited. Kathleen didn't know if the two young people were officially courting, but it was a friendship she was keen to encourage, having seen the way Leonie's face lit up at the sight of Kenny's letter or the mention of her nephew.

"I wish you could come with us, but the doctors believe it will set back your progress."

"I know, and I think they are right. I get very tired. Here I have a routine, and I can stick to it. I can get to the hospital to see my doctors. I'm sure there are doctors in Riverside Springs or at least in nearby towns, but they might not have the same expertise." Leonie clasped her hands in her lap. "It is better I get well and not be a burden on anyone."

"Nobody believes you would be a burden."

Leonie glanced at Kathleen but then looked back at her hands. "There is another reason I would prefer you to be on the train. I promised Maria I would help her with fundraising, and I spoke to a reporter. He wrote a story which he wants to publish in his newspaper."

Kathleen's breath caught in her throat. She exchanged a look with her husband; they both remembered the abuse Johanna Chiver had suffered, before her gaze returned to Leonie.

"But what about your father? He might read it and find out about your mother's death and come looking for you."

Leonie's lips thinned "I thought of that, but the families of the shirtwaist factory victims need help, and if I can raise money by selling my story, I am going to do that. My father... no that man doesn't deserve that title, Mr. Chiver can do what he likes. If the children have already gone, he can't touch them. I will tell him they have been adopted, and there is nothing he can do. I won't have anything to do with him."

"But if he insists?"

"I won't live in fear any longer. I've had plenty of time to think about everything, and I refuse to let anyone control my actions. Especially a man like him."

"That's something I will drink to." Inspector Griffin raised his teacup. "If that man crawls out of the woodwork, please call on my services."

Richard nodded. "And mine. I can testify to what your mother suffered at his hands."

Richard walked across the room to put his hand on Kathleen's shoulder. "Well my dear, are you convinced? Will you go to Riverside Springs?"

Kathleen nodded, wiping away tears from her eyes. She was so lucky to have such a wonderful husband and amazing friends.

# CHAPTER 16

*L*ily reached up to pick a leaf from the Hawthorn tree.

"Don't touch. For the love of all things sacred, keep your hands away from the tree. It's a fairy tree," Deirdre pulled at Lily's dress as the words tumbled out of her mouth. Lily couldn't get over the look of fear on the child's face.

"I won't touch, I promise. But what do you mean it's a fairy tree?"

"See?" Deirdre pointed to a ring-shaped mound in the grass that Lily hadn't seen. "That's a fairy fort. We know never to touch it or walk on it. The little folk live there, and they don't like it when we come to visit. We must leave. Now." Deirdre pulled Lily's hand. To placate the child, Lily followed her. When the child stopped moving so fast, Lily leaned down so that she was level with her face. "I'm sorry, Deirdre, I didn't mean any harm. I just needed a walk."

"I know you didn't do it on purpose, but the fairies, they might be mad, and then Daddy will have more to worry about."

"Oh, your poor child." Lily swept the child up into her arms as tears flowed down Deirdre's face.

"I heard Mammy and Daddy arguing last night. The fairies must have made the cow go dry and the hens stop laying eggs."

"No, darling, the fox got two of your mother's best laying hens. She told me so herself."

Deirdre gave Lily a look suggesting she was a fool to believe that.

"It's the little people. They send lots of bad luck when they get upset with you."

"Sweetheart, your parents have had some bad luck. All families go through a time when everything seems to turn out bad, but then things change, and good things happen."

Deirdre brightened up. "Do you think we

should leave a present for the fairies? That might help to change things."

Lily wasn't sure if she should let the child believe in such things.

"Who told you about the fairies and their trees and homes?"

Deirdre sighed. "Everyone knows about fairies in Ireland."

Lily laughed. "Well, I don't know anything, so why don't you tell me what you think they might like as a present."

Deirdre eyed Lily's coat.

"My coat?" Lily prompted when the child remained silent.

"No, not the coat. They don't need clothes. But they like shiny things, and your buttons are silver-colored. Maybe they wouldn't be mad anymore if you gave them a button."

Lily pushed aside the thought that this was perhaps the silliest thing she had ever done. If it made Deirdre happier, then it was worth it. She bit the threads securing the button to her coat sleeve. Releasing the button, she handed it to the child.

"What do we do next?"

"We have to walk very quietly back up to

the tree and place the button under it. Then we must leave just as quietly. If we hear them sing, it means they accept the gift."

Singing fairies! Lily hid a smile and tried to look as if she was taking the child seriously.

"I'll follow you; you are quieter than me."

Deirdre walked very slowly, picking out her steps carefully. Lily tried her best to follow along. Then she watched as the child kissed the button before placing it on the ground under the tree. The child whispered something, but Lily couldn't hear what she said. Deirdre turned to Lily, putting her finger to her mouth so that Lily didn't speak and taking Lily's hand led her a short distance away.

Deirdre held her head to one side, listening intently. Then she smiled. "Can you hear them?"

Lily listened. She couldn't hear a thing but a cow mooing in the distance.

"Can you, Miss Lily?"

"I hear something."

Deirdre nodded, a look of satisfaction on her face. "That's them singing. They are happy now. Good luck will come to Daddy and

Mammy. I know it. Let's go home and tell them."

The child looked up at Lily, the trusting look on her face making her want to cry. Instead, she forced a smile. "I think that's a good idea, Deirdre. You lead the way."

# CHAPTER 17

*I*n the end, Kathleen decided to leave Richie and Esme at home in New York. She took her seat on the train with Nettie sitting on her right and Carrie on her left. Miss Cooper sat opposite, with the children spread among the eight rows of seats. Mr. Forrester, a member of the Orphan Train Society, accompanied them to see to the boys. Kathleen wasn't sure what to make of Forrester. He seemed pleasant enough but had an air of being disinterested in the whole proceedings and spent his time reading rather than interacting with the children. Miss Cooper was a natural; the children flocked to her side as she told them stories, giving one or two a cuddle when they looked a bit glum.

The train itself hadn't changed much from the one Kathleen had taken all those years ago in her quest to find her brothers. She closed her eyes, seeing Patrick as the orphan he had been back then. Now she had letters in her bag from her adult son, a doctor in London who was finding his new life most entertaining. Frieda had also written, telling her of how useful Lily had been in setting up their new household and making her laugh at the house-keeper's attempts to get them to maintain the class divide between mistress and servant. Something Lily and Frieda took no notice of whatsoever. Kathleen wondered if Richard and herself would ever get to visit London. Would her husband be able to take time off from his job? Maybe they could sail on the Titanic to Southampton. Lily would dock in New York on April 17th, about seven days after Kathleen would land in Riverside Springs. She hoped Lily would understand why she had taken the trip.

"Will you be there when we meet our new parents, Miss Kathleen?"

"Yes, Nettie, I will."

"What if we don't like them or they don't like us?"

Kathleen pulled the little girl onto her lap and cuddled her, sensing her fear. "Sweetheart, they couldn't help but love you and your brother. From what they have written, they seem to be very nice people. My sister, Bridget, is a good judge of character and she likes them."

Nettie sucked on her thumb.

"But it will take a while for you to get used to them and them to you. You can't expect to love them straight away."

"I loved you the minute I saw you. I knew you were kind and would be a good mother. Why can't we stay with you?" The child looked up at her, her eyes wide, and her lower lip trembled.

Kathleen pushed her hair back from her eyes. "I wish you could, Nettie, but you and Max need a home together where you will be the center of your parents' attention. My husband is very busy at the hospital with all the sick people who need his help to get better. I must look after other children who come to the sanctuary as well as my own two."

Nettie clung closer to Kathleen. "So long as that's the truth. I thought it might be because you didn't like us."

"Never think that, Nettie. Elmer and Pearl Haverford are the luckiest people to have got the pair of you as their children."

The boys were fascinated by the steam engine pulling the train, commenting on the clouds of steam and smoke billowing into the air as they made their way to Wyoming. Several times, Kathleen had to remind them to stay away from the front engines when the train made stops to stock up on fuel and water. These stops gave the children a chance to stretch their legs, and if long enough, time to venture into a small town to replenish their provisions. Kathleen was saddened to see that the attitudes of the townspeople toward the orphans hadn't changed much from her previous visit. Some people were friendly, but most made a point of walking away from the children as if they were carriers of contagious diseases. More than one parent pulled their child back when curiosity got the better of them. Kathleen saw that Miss Cooper noticed the same. The younger woman made a point of leading the children in silly songs to distract them. Before they entered the town store, Miss Cooper divided the children into groups of five and admonished them to behave before escorting them inside. Kathleen looked on proudly as the young woman excelled at keeping the children in check. She had been right; Miss Cooper had been born for this job.

The train pulled into Green River, a pretty town named for the river, an important waterway for the region. The train station served as a hub connecting eastern and western parts of America, and business seemed to be booming with plenty of hotels, restaurants, saloons, stores, as well as laundries and other service providers to suit both the travelers and the locals. Many men were employed in the maintenance facilities and repair shops needed for the railway, but agriculture and livestock farming also played a role in the town's economy. Several of the children traveling in their party would find families among the ranchers, while others would remain in town, learning the trades of their new fathers.

Kathleen saw the conflicting emotions play out on Miss Cooper's face. She understood that the young woman was torn between being thrilled that some orphans would find good homes and knowing that there would be some who would be disappointed. Kathleen would never forget her first experience with showing orphans to a town; it had reminded her of an animal auction, only instead of people inspecting livestock, they had come up on the stage demanding to see the insides of children's mouths and raising their arms and legs to see if they were healthy. Kathleen stood taller; she was determined that there would be none of that happening tomorrow. These children would be treated with respect.

She escorted the group through the busy streets toward the Whitewater hotel. The hosts were known to the Orphan Train society, and while the accommodations were basic, they were clean, and the children were provided with baths and comfortable beds. Mr. and Mrs. Klein, a German couple, had previously adopted children from the train. They displayed their children's portraits on the walls of their hotel.

Mrs. Klein came out to greet them, wearing a white apron tied around her bulky middle. "Come in, kinder, I have made you some special cookies. But first, you must wash your hands and eat some stew with potatoes. It will make you big and strong, grow hairs on your chest. Yes." Mrs. Klein nodded as she smiled at each child. When her eyes met Kathleen's, they opened in wonder.

"Miss Kathleen? It is you. I thought I might be dreaming. You don't look a day older than the last time you came here."

Kathleen laughed as the woman engulfed her in a warm hug. "You were always short-sighted, Mrs. Klein, and far too kind. I'm not that naïve young girl anymore. I have grey hair now."

"We all have some grey hairs. But you are happy, I can see it in your eyes. The years have been good to you. But why am I speaking to you in the street like a tramp? Come inside. All of you."

Kathleen gestured to Miss Cooper to follow her inside, Mr. Forrester having already taken a seat at one of the tables set for their party.

"You go to see your sister, Mrs. Vatson?"

Kathleen ignored the mispronunciation. "Yes. I can't wait to see her and her family and of course Shane, Angel, and their family. It will be like going home." Kathleen helped Nettie and Carrie with their napkins before taking her own seat, her stomach grumbling at the appetizing smells coming from the large pots sitting on the serving board.

Mrs. Klein ladled large amounts of stew into the bowls and placed one in front of each child. Mr. Klein nodded to Kathleen before returning to check on the other customers in the front dining room. Kathleen was glad the children had the back room to themselves. They didn't have to endure being stared at as they ate.

"How is life with you, Mrs. Klein? Is business good?"

"Ya, very good. We have nothing to complain about. And who would listen if we did." Mrs. Klein laughed as she playfully pinched Carrie's cheek. "You look like a little princess with your lovely hair."

Carrie beamed.

"Green River is so busy now, the trains come faster and faster, bigger and bigger. And the streets, the motor cars, they make so much noise. My ears ring when I go to the store. But it is a good place to live. The churches are full on Sundays, not just our own one but all of them. The people are mostly good. A few bad eggs like everywhere else, but it is a good place."

"Your children have grown up."

Mrs. Klein's smile almost split her face in two. "Yes, my Felix and Marion, they are all grown up. Marion is married and is having a baby in three months. I will be a grandma at last. Felix, he is courting a young lady but he is also taking exams and trying to build a business. Busy, busy man. See children, look at how happy two children just like you made me. You are blessings from God, and never forget that."

Kathleen caught Miss Cooper's gaze and smiled. If only all the adoptive parents were like Mrs. Klein. She closed down those thoughts straight away.

After every child had eaten as much as they wanted, they were given a bath and put to bed in clean nightclothes. Their new clothes, the ones they would wear to meet their prospective parents the next morning, were arranged in the closet in each room. Kathleen and Miss Cooper read the younger children stories, giving out hugs as required. To her surprise, Mr. Forrester volunteered to help the Kleins tidy up after the dinner. Only when everything was clean and tidy once more did he retire to a corner with his book.

Kathleen took advantage of the children being asleep to speak to Miss Cooper.

"Tomorrow will be difficult, not just for the children. I still remember my first time witnessing prospective families inspect the children. For that is what some of them did."

Miss Cooper took a sip of her coffee before replacing the cup on the table. "I heard some stories back in the orphanage. Some orphans had been placed in families and ran away, preferring to live at the asylum. They didn't have good tales to tell."

Kathleen wasn't about to sugarcoat the truth. "In truth, although we want to match children to families who will take them in and raise them like their own, like the Kleins have, the reality is that it doesn't always work out that way. Just as some people aren't good parents to their natural children, there are those who see the orphans as cheap labor for their farms or stores. We try to avoid the worst of these situations. For example, we never allow unmarried men to adopt." Kathleen squirmed a little. Although Miss Cooper had worked in the hospital, she was still innocent. Or at least she hoped she was, although by the blush forming on the younger woman's cheeks, she probably knew more than some girls of a similar age.

"For some of the children, like Max and Nettie, we have arranged adoptions in advance. For others, they will meet their parents tomorrow. Every prospective adoptive parent should have a reference from their church leader. Father Nelson would have a fit if he heard me say this, but I still say to trust your gut instinct. A person can be a saint in a church but an evil person in the privacy of their own home. If you don't like the way anyone handles the children, let me know."

Miss Cooper nodded.

"Mrs. Klein will accompany us too. She knows many of the townsfolk, so she is a good sounding board."

"I just hope the children who are looking

for new homes in Green River find them. I
don't want them to be disappointed."

Kathleen squeezed Miss Cooper's hand.
"You have a very kind heart. Never lose that,
my dear."

# CHAPTER 18

$\mathcal{L}$ily sat on a wall, looking out at the green fields surrounding the Doherty farm. She could smell the seaweed in the air, hear the roar of the waves from the sea. It was so beautiful and peaceful. If you listened carefully, you could hear the birds singing, animals scuttling from one place to the next. But it was partly a mirage, this peaceful scene. She sensed the tension, the anxiety of the women working in the farmhouses, wondering whether they would have sufficient funds to keep their family together. Or would their children follow the path of their ancestors, leaving for foreign parts in search of a better life?

"There you are. You look miles away," Charlie's voice made her jump; she hadn't seen him approach. "Are you all right?"

"I was just thinking how sad it is that the young people of Ireland have to leave such a beautiful place. Everyone we speak to has family living in America or England. Few seem to leave because they have a yearning to see the world, but instead, they have to go. They can't stay living at home because there isn't enough money to keep them. The farms are so small, yet the families are large."

Charlie took her hand. "Please don't upset yourself, Lily. There is nothing we can do to change things."

Lily turned on him. "But we must try. At least to help Niamh and Tom. They are your family. We spend all our time helping people in New York, but here your family is nearly just as badly off. Niamh is worried sick about her sons and how they may get involved in the Irish struggle."

"Tom is happy for his boys to be involved."

"Niamh isn't. She told me about her grandfather. He was convicted of being a member of the Fenian movement and transported to

Australia. Her grandmother was left to fend for herself and her children. The man didn't even own a weapon, and yet he was sentenced to penal servitude, never to see his family again. How is that fair?"

Tom swiped at a fly that had landed on his cheek. "I never said it was," he grumbled. "She is bitter over what happened, and she has reason to be, but the British haven't transported anyone to Australia or anywhere else for some time. Horrible things happened back then, but there was fault on both sides. John Taylor knew it was against the law to join the Fenians. He knew the consequences."

"His family was starving. What was he supposed to do?" Lily retorted.

"I don't know, but why are we arguing about this now? For all I know, my own family was probably in the same movement. Gran believes in Ireland being a free country. So do I, but I can't change what happened to Niamh's grandfather."

She'd upset him, and it wasn't fair. It wasn't Charlie's fault. "I'm sorry. I just get so annoyed thinking about what your people have been through. Those English families living in their grand houses and the Irish are living below the poverty line."

Charlie took her hand in his. "You sound like a proper revolutionary."

Hurt, she pulled away. "Don't mock me."

"Lily, I was joking. Don't you think I feel the same? It was my family who had to leave their home or die from starvation. Gran would do anything to see this place again."

She stared at him, not knowing what to say.

He leaned in and cupped her face with his hands. "I think all the talk last night of Home Rule and the Fianna upset us both. But let's not fight."

She kissed him. "I'm sorry, it's me being moody. I just wish there was something we could do to help Tom and Niamh. They have been so gracious to us, and it's obvious they are struggling."

"They have their pride, Lily. You saw the way Niamh reacted when I brought those items from the store. She nearly took the head off me."

Lily chuckled. "She does have a real Irish temper. I can see her and Kathleen getting into an argument, and all the dishes around them being sent flying into smithereens." Lily traced the lines on his hands. "But there must be something we can do. Niamh mentioned they are in arrears on their rent and that they could lose the farm. If that happens, what would they live on? Should we ask them to come and live with us?"

"Come to America? Weren't you just saying that it's horrible for people to have to leave this island?"

Lily sighed, feeling conflicted. "What else is there?"

He offered her his arm, and together they strolled back in the direction of the farm.

"What if you were to loan Tom the money to clear the rent arrears? We could replace the hens Niamh lost to the foxes? That way, she would have eggs to sell again at the market."

"Don't you think I have thought of that? But what happens when the next harvest is poor? The reality is that the farm is too small, and the land too poor to make a real go of it. Tom needs more acres to feed his family and pay his landlord."

They walked along in silence. There had to be an answer. They couldn't just get on the

Titanic and sail back to New York and leave the lovely Doherty family in despair. She knew Charlie wouldn't want to do that.

"Are you ready to go home?" Charlie asked, taking her hand in his. "Excited to see the children? See how the factory is progressing?"

"Of course, I can't wait to see the children; I've missed them so much. I'm sure the factory is thriving under Gustav and Conrad's care. I hope Kathleen hasn't been working too hard; it was a lot to ask her to take care of everything."

"But?"

Lily turned to look at him. "I'm scared of going back." There, she'd said it. She looked away, out over the coast, watching the waves crash against the shore. "Here I can forget about all the horrible things that happened over the last few years. I can sleep without having nightmares about the fire. I'm afraid when I get back to New York, I'll feel helpless all over again."

He put his arms around her, drawing her to his chest. "Darling, you have never been helpless. Not since that first day I met you. None of what happened was your fault. If not for you, Kathleen, Frieda, Maria, Anne Morgan, and several other incredible women, the cost of those tragedies would have been much higher. I understand it is difficult to return to New York, but we both have so much more to do."

"What will you do? You said you wouldn't practice law again after that court case."

"That was a decision taken in haste. It's a bit pointless having worked so hard for my degree not to use it. As you constantly point out, there are far too many people who try to take advantage of others. I'm well placed to help those who wish to help themselves."

"So, you will return to the office?"

"Yes, and thankfully they want me to come back. The senior partners recognized I was overworked. They told me the day I was leaving that they would keep my position for me for six months."

Lily eyed her husband closely. "Why didn't you tell me?"

"I was too angry to even consider it, and I thought by telling you, you might try to influence me. I know that was a stupid thing to think. You have never pushed me to do anything."

Lily leaned into his shoulder. "I'm glad you are going back to work."

"You are?" He mumbled, kissing the back of her ear. "I thought you liked having me all to yourself."

Lily flushed, even though nobody could hear him. "I do, but you would have been bored out of your mind and getting under my feet in no time at all."

"I don't think I could ever get bored of you." He nuzzled the area near her collar bone in a very distracting fashion. She blushed when Deirdre came running out to greet them.

"Lily you're back. Come and see what I made. Mammy is showing me how to make lace just like her." Deirdre pulled Lily toward the door. "Dinner is almost ready. We're just waiting for Daddy to get back from the field."

# CHAPTER 19

"When are you leaving Sligo?" Tom asked as he picked up two large potatoes and placed them on his plate. Using his fork, he made a space for some butter. He added a twist of salt and only then did he start eating.

Charlie swallowed the food he'd been chewing. "On Wednesday we head for Cork where we will join the Titanic when it docks at Queenstown on Thursday. We should be back in New York the following Wednesday."

"The Titanic? Did I read somewhere they have a swimming pool on that ship?" Tom speared another potato on to his plate.

"Aye in first class along with several suites,

restaurants and other malarky. It's like a floating palace from what I hear. There's many an American wake planned for this Saturday." Niamh dished out some vegetables insisting the children ate them despite the look on their faces.

Niamh glanced up at Lily. "There's a family in the village whose son Paddy is heading away. You can come with us to the wake."

Lily wasn't sure she wanted to go, it sounded so morbid.

Tom caught the look on her face. "It's a way of people to deal with their sadness but they also give the people leaving happy memories of home. The drinks will be flowing and the women will cook up a spread. It's great craic for everyone."

Niamh stood and started clearing the dishes from the table "Aye aside from the poor woman saying goodbye to her child. Mary Martha will never see her Paddy again and he, her youngest. She wanted him to join the priesthood, but young Paddy has his mind set on seeing the world." Niamh finished her own meal, pushing the plate to one side. She lifted a glass full of buttermilk and took a long drink.

"That's not all he has his mind set on. A tom cat would be better behaved."

Niamh spluttered. "Tom Doherty, mind your language in front of the children." But despite her tone, Niamh kissed the top of his head as she passed by him.

"Will you stay here tonight. There's a storm brewing, you can hear it in the wind."

Charlie glanced at Lily. She'd prefer to sleep in her bed at Widow O'Reilly's house but left the decision to him.

"We better not. Mrs. O'Reilly is expecting us and she might worry if we don't go back. And I borrowed the horse and cart from Frank, he may have need of it tomorrow."

"Aye true that."

ONCE FINISHED, the men withdrew to the chairs beside the fire leaving the women to clean up. They were deep in conversation when Lily finished and stood near Charlie.

"There must be a way to help, Tom. I know you won't take charity but with my business contacts and your knowledge of farming, between the two of us, we should think of something."

"What about cows?"

The men turned to look at Lily who refused to look guilty at eavesdropping on their conversation.

"What do you mean?" Charlie asked.

"I've seen men pushing cows off the ships in New York. Lots of them. There must be some money in that. You have the farming knowledge and Charlie knows plenty of businesses. Do you remember Charlie when Mr. Prentice had problems getting his meat and our friends in Clover Springs were able to help."

Charlie looked baffled but there was a gleam in Tom's eye. A spark of hope. "Cattle dealers work from all the ports in Ireland. They send live cattle across the ocean to the slaughterhouses. Irish cattle provide good quality meat." The light dimmed in his eyes as his voice fell. "It would be a costly operation to set up."

Lily wasn't about to give up. "But you don't need to start big, do you? Couldn't you try it on a smaller scale first. Maybe one of your sons could get a job with a cattle dealer to find out what's involved. It might be worth a shot. Mr. Prentice will help; I know he will."

Charlie beamed, stood up and putting his arm around her shoulders, "Lily you are a genius."

"No, I'm not. It was just an idea. It might not work. Come back to the table and let's talk about it. Niamh made more tea and a cake."

Tom rubbed his chin, deep in thought. Lily and Charlie sat in silence. Once Niamh sat down, she spoke up. "We could give it a try. It would be a way to get Declan away from all that union and rebellion talk. Young men like adventure, crossing the ocean would be nothing to him. Frank Reilly would likely lend a hand if you asked him."

"I don't want charity, woman."

Stung, Niamh's temper flared. "I don't want to bury any more of my family. Enough is enough. You have the chance now of help. Take it you stubborn old man or I swear I'll…." Niamh pushed the chair back as she stood and ran out of the cottage. Tom went to stand but Lily said, "I'll go."

Lily grabbed Niamh's shawl and followed her out to the barn where she found the woman leaning against the wall, her head in her hands, shoulders shaking.

Lily wrapped the shawl around the woman's shoulders. Niamh looked up. "I never once spoke to my Tom like that before I don't know what came over me. You'll go back to America thinking all I do is storm out of the house. I don't know why I'm acting like this."

Lily rubbed Niamh's arm. "You are worried, that's all. He knows you didn't mean any harm. He's a good man, just caught in a bad place. He can't see any way out of his troubles and like most men, he lets his pride get in the way."

"Aye but we can't live on pride."

Lily pushed Niamh to comment further. "What do you think of the idea? Do you know any cattle dealers?"

"No but Frank Reilly will. He knows everyone."

Lily gave Niamh a nudge. "Maybe you could go back in and make that suggestion. Instead of a two way deal between Charlie and Tom, maybe they could do a three way deal with Frank Reilly. He has the contacts here, Tom has the knowledge of cattle and Charlie has contacts in New York."

Niamh rubbed her eyes. "Tom won't like it. Not coming from a woman."

Lily stayed quiet, not wanting to contradict or criticize. Niamh gave her a look. "Still it's my family too. You're right."

They walked back together to the cottage. Lily gestured for Charlie that it was time to leave. "Tom and Niamh have things to talk about. Let's leave them to it. Thank you for the lovely meal. We will see you on Saturday."

"Aye and tell Widow O'Reilly you will stay here the night. That way we can have a few drinks and not be worried about you leading the horse astray."

Tom's joke fell flat. Lily gave him a smile but forced laughter at his words did nothing to dampen the rising tension in the room.

* * *

As CHARLIE DROVE Frank's wagon back to Sligo, Lily watched him closely. "You're excited about this aren't you?"

"Yes. It's a way to help Tom and Niamh but it's more than that Lily." Charlie stopped the wagon and turned to her, a gleam of excitement in his eyes. "I love it here. I didn't expect to but I do. The pace of life is slower than at home in New York. I'm not saying I want to live here but I want to bring our family back to see this place. To see where they came from. To hear the history, the good and the bad. Does that make any sense?"

"Yes it does. You feel the pull of belonging. I don't have that but you always had a connection with Ireland. It started from the stories Carmel used to tell you when you were young."

Charlie nodded in agreement. "You're right, it did. All those old stories of the warriors. Grainne the pirate queen, Cu Chulainn, the children of Lir, all of it. And this place, it is so, so beautiful."

Lily waited for him to continue but he seemed hesitant.

"What is it Charlie?"

"I'm not sure if my dreams and yours are on the same path."

Shocked she stared at him. "What does that mean?"

"You are totally committed to Carmel's Mission and I understand that. I married you knowing that is the life you wanted and for years, I was happy with that. But lately, the toil of the endless misery, the poverty, corruption, strikes, deaths, they are eating into you Lily. Destroying you bit by bit and I'm terrified we are losing you. Being here in Ireland, with you and just you, it's given me a taste of what life would be like without the sanctuary and the orphan trains. Just you, me and our children."

Lily opened her mouth, but he put his finger on her lips to silence her. "I look at Tom and Niamh, I know they are struggling but aside from her outburst tonight they are fully committed to each other. I want that, Lily." He looked her in the eyes "Do you?"

She couldn't help looking away, she wasn't at all sure if she was telling the truth even as she said the words, "I am committed to you. How could you think otherwise?"

He stared into the distance for so long she wasn't sure he had heard her. Then he turned, the look of sadness in his eyes hitting her right in the heart. "But we aren't enough for you Lily, are we? The children and I? You need the sanctuary. You aren't happy unless you are off saving someone." He clicked the reins and the wagon lurched as they set off for the guesthouse.

The wind grew stronger as they drove back into Sligo, the rain pouring down as if it would never stop. Freezing and wet through to her undergarments, Lily was relieved to see the guesthouse. Charlie motioned for her to go inside. "I'll just take the horse round the back to the stables. You go on before you catch a chill."

Lily didn't need to be told twice. She walked up the path and through the front door, where Maeve greeted her.

"Tis a nasty night. Thank God you are back. Would you like a cup of tea and a slice of cake?"

Lily had got used to drinking tea. "Thank you Maeve that would be lovely. I'm just going to go and change. We got caught in the downpour." Lily went upstairs to the bedroom glad to see the fire had been lit and the room was warm. She changed quickly expecting to see Charlie arrive in any second but he had still not appeared when she went back downstairs.

"Wasn't Charlie with you?' Maeve asked as she served up the tea.

"Yes. He said he was just taking the horse

around to the stable. Knowing him he is giving the poor animal a good rub down and some oats."

"Pity Frank is still down the pub or he could have done that for him."

Time passed by with Maeve keeping Lily entertained with stories of her neighbors but Lily began to feel uneasy. Where was Charlie?

She stood up. "I think I should go and check on Charlie."

"You stay here, you don't know your way and the path is a bit uneven. I'll go."

Lily protested but the woman insisted. She watched as the widow grabbed a shawl and disappeared out the back door. She wasn't gone long. "Lily, bring a blanket. Charlie is fine but he hurt his leg and his head. I must go find Frank. I'll be back as soon as I can."

Lily lifted her skirts and ran with the cup of tea in her hand, out to where Charlie lay sprawled across the stable floor. "Charlie what happened?" Lily quickly covered him with the blanket, feeling his body shaking with the cold.

"Something spooked the horse, he reared up and crashed into me." Charlie's voice shook as his teeth chattered together. "I think my ankle is broken and I'll have a headache in the morning."

Lily pulled off the shawl she had borrowed and folded it under his head. Then she looked down at his feet, his left ankle was swelling. She wondered if she should remove his shoe.

But then she heard the voices, recognizing Frank and Maeve's. "Help is coming darling."

Frank put a splint around Charlie's injured leg before he and four of his friends carried him into the house. Maeve insisted they put him on the couch in the front room.

"I sent the Mahony lad for the doctor. He needs to see to him. I'll go and make him a nice cup of tea." Maeve turned to leave.

"It's whiskey he needs woman and not tea."

"Sweet Tea is good for the shock." Maeve retorted excusing herself to go to the kitchen.

Frank ignored her and helping Charlie to a seated position, he handed him a small flask. "Get that into you. It will help with the pain. What happened?"

"I don't know really. Something spooked the horse. She reared up and then she stepped back, her hoof hitting my leg. I didn't see anything, it was too dark."

"I should have been here to see to the horse."

Maeve contradicted him. "Frank you didn't know what time they would be back. You're not to blame. Here's the doctor now."

The doctor was a young man, recently qualified and back from London. He reminded Lily of Patrick with the same caring bedside manner. "You're a lucky man. It's a clean break but part of the bone came through the skin so we will have to keep an eye on it to check for infection. We will have to splint it and you must not put any weight on it. Bed rest for the first week or so at least."

"Bed rest? I can't do that. We travel on the Titanic on the 11th." Even as he spoke, Charlie winced with the pain, his face pale against the couch.

The doctor shook his head. "Sorry Mr. Doherty but you won't be fit to sail by then. All things going well, you should be set to go home by the middle of June." The doctor turned to Maeve. "A poultice for the swelling may help with the pain and prevent infection setting in. I will leave you some morphine but use it sparingly."

"Yes Doctor, thank you."

Lily knew she should be the one dealing with the doctor, but she wasn't fit for more than holding Charlie's hand. If the horse had caught him on the head or he'd cracked his skull when he'd fallen. Anything could have happened.

"Lily drink this, you're as white as a corpse. Charlie will be fine. The men will help carry him up the stairs to your bedroom. Of course, the both of you are welcome to stay until he is ready to go home. Tomorrow you can go to the post office and send a telegram or letter to your family. But in the meantime, get this down you." Lily took the cup of sweetened tea, her hands shaking as she lifted it to her mouth. She took a deep drink before setting it back on the small table. The men rallied around Charlie, helping to move him up the stairs to the bedroom. She couldn't bear to watch having seen Charlie bite his lip when they jarred his foot.

As Charlie lay on the bed drifting in and out of consciousness, Lily nursed him. She kept giving him small amount of water as per the doctor's orders. She watched as Maeve made up the poultice for his ankle.

"This will help reduce the swelling and that will help with the pain. Lily you need to get some rest. It wont do any good you falling ill as well. I will sit with him for a time, you go and lie down in the next room. I made it up for you. It is best to let him sleep alone so you don't kick his ankle in your sleep."

"But I want to be here when he wakes up."

"The morphine will have him drifting in and out for the next forty eight hours. Go on lass, you have nothing to fear. You heard the doctor, he is not in any danger. The only thing he will die from is boredom."

Reluctantly Lily did as she was told. Instead of resting, she sat at the writing desk in the second room, staring at the writing paper. How did she tell their children they wouldn't be returning to New York any time soon. Would it really be June before Charlie was able to travel? Kathleen would look after the children so she knew they would be safe but they'd worry. Especially tender hearted Grace who was very close to her father. Lily gave up thoughts of writing and buried her head in her hands and cried. She must have fallen asleep as she woke up with her head on the desk, a creak in her neck. She washed her face with the cold water from the basin before going next door to check on Charlie.

"He's still sleeping. But he woke earlier and had some soup."

"Earlier? How long was I asleep?"

"About three hours. You look better for it too." Maeve stood and picked up the tray. "I'll leave you to it now. I'll check on him later but come and get me if you need anything."

"Thank you, Maeve. You didn't bargain for this when you took our booking."

"Tis nothing. You'd do the same yourself if the shoe was on the other foot."

Lily sat on the edge of the bed making sure to stay away from his bad ankle. She moved the hair from his eyes, checking the purple-colored bruises on the side of his face. He must have hit the wall with some force. She couldn't bear to think of what could have happened. She stayed by his side for hours but aside from muttering and wincing in his sleep, he didn't wake up.

. . .

THE NEXT MORNING, Charlie was wide awake and sitting up in bed when Lily came in. Tears of relief made her eyes sting.

"Don't cry. I'm fine just feeling a bit silly. I'm sorry you will miss the crossing. I promised you the trip of a lifetime."

"I don't care about any of that. I'm just glad you weren't hurt too badly. What if the horse had caught your head?"

He took her hand in his, playing with her fingers. "The horse had more sense. He knew he would get hurt on my old noggin."

She smiled at his attempt at a joke. As she watched, his eyes fluttered. She leaned in and gave him a kiss. "Sleep darling. Maeve and the doctor said it was the best thing for you."

# CHAPTER 20

*T*he low rumble of a steam locomotive woke Kathleen the next morning. She yawned, gasping from the cold as her feet hit the wooden floors. Although it was early April, the morning air was chilly. Glancing out the window, she saw it was a dry day with the sun rising on the horizon, the sky a pretty mix of blues and pinks, hopefully heralding a good day ahead. She dressed quickly, lured by the smell of freshly brewed coffee wafting up the stairs. The sounds from the surrounding rooms indicated the children were waking. Kathleen checked the girls' rooms to ensure even the sleepiest were up and dressed. They would enjoy a good breakfast, those who weren't too nervous to eat, before making their way to the town hall to meet prospective parents. Crossing herself, Kathleen said a quick prayer that everything would work out well.

She led the procession to the town hall, holding Nettie and Carrie's hands. Miss Cooper followed at the rear, with Mr. Forrester having gone ahead to ensure everything was set up correctly in the hall. Mrs. Klein had promised to follow as soon as the last of her guests had eaten breakfast.

"Do I still look clean?" Nettie asked as they walked past the stores.

"Yes, of course you do," Kathleen reassured her with a smile. "Nettie, they will love you."

Nettie didn't look convinced, and her mood wasn't helped when Carrie piped up, "I'm so glad I'm going with you to Riverside Springs. I don't want to say goodbye to you today."

Kathleen groaned as Nettie began to cry. She bent down, picking the young girl up. "Dry your tears, Nettie. You and Max will be together. I promise I will write to you."

"I'm sorry, Nettie, I didn't mean to make you cry," Carrie said before bursting into tears herself. Kathleen put Nettie on the ground and gathered both girls into a big hug. "Dry your eyes, good girls."

A woman in her early thirties, dressed in a well-worn plain cotton dress and a bonnet protecting her face, quickened her step toward them. "Can I help? I'm good with children. Poor little things are finding it all rather over-whelming," she offered.

Kathleen saw the kindness in the stranger's green eyes, noted how her calloused hands gently pushed auburn tendrils of hair away from her face.

"These girls are good friends and are a little sad about being separated today," Kathleen explained.

The woman smiled at the girls. "Maybe you can write to one another. Then when you are a bit older you might be able to meet up one day. What are your names?"

"I'm Carrie and that's Nettie."

"Nettie?" The woman's eyes widened as she glanced at Kathleen and then back to Nettie.

"My name is Pearl Haverford. My husband

Elmer and I are here to adopt a girl called Nettie and her brother Max. Is that you?"

Nettie nodded but her grip on Kathleen's hand grew tighter. Mrs. Haverford's smile grew wider. "It's delightful to meet you Nettie and you too Carrie. If Nettie decides to come with me to live in our home, I promise to help her write letters to her friends."

Kathleen watched Nettie's reaction but the child simply stared at Mrs. Haverford.

"I'm Kathleen Green, Mrs. Haverford."

The woman held out her hand to shake Kathleen's. She had a firm honest grip. Kathleen liked what she had seen so far. "Why don't we make our way inside and find Max. He went ahead with Miss Cooper to help her take care of a couple of the other boys who are a little homesick for New York."

Mrs. Haverford fell into step beside Kathleen. "It must be very difficult for them to leave all they have known and come out here to strangers. My heart breaks for them but I have read stories of how dangerous the streets of New York are and I have to believe they are better off being taken away from the city."

"They are. In most cases that is." Kathleen

RACHEL WESSON

corrected herself softly. "Some of the children who are here today will accompany us to Riverside Springs. I believe you know my sister, Bridget Watson."

Mrs. Haverford nodded. "I should have probably waited until you arrived in Riverside Springs. Elmer kept telling me that was the correct thing to do but I was just too excited."

Nettie broke free of Kathleen's hand to run to Max when they entered the hall. Mrs. Haverford took a step to move closer to them but Kathleen put a hand on her arm. "I think you should take things a little more slowly with Max. Although he is only seven, he has been protecting Nettie and providing for her for almost a full year since their mother was killed in the Triangle Shirtwaist fire. He adored his mother and so is struggling with the idea of replacing her."

Mrs. Haverford looked stricken with guilt. "I don't wish to replace her. I thought I made that clear in the letter."

"You did. But from Max's perspective he doesn't know you and his recent experiences haven't done anything to endear strangers to

236

him." Kathleen bit her lip for a second wondering should she tell the woman about the prison cell. She decided honesty was the best policy. "Max was arrested recently through no fault of his own. He was badly treated by the police and ended up in hospital. I'm afraid it has made him even less trusting than he was after the aunt ran off and left them to fend for themselves."

"The poor boy." Mrs. Haverford folded her arms. "I want to gather them both up and hug them tight and promise that nothing bad is ever going to happen to them again. But I can't do that. I have no control over such things. If I did our twins would still be alive."

"I'm sorry for your loss, Mrs. Haverford."

Mrs. Haverford wiped a tear from her eye. "Pearl please. It was a long time ago. While we will never get over losing our boys, we have learned to deal with the pain. We have so much love to give Mrs. Green, so much. My Elmer, he walks tall and to some he looks so solemn but you should hear him laugh. He built things for our boys, swings and other toys for them to play with. He put them away, you know … after."

"Does he feel the same as you do? Is he ready to open his home to children?"

Pearl nodded. "His home and his heart, that I promise you. I know you will send inspectors to visit us in a year's time. I give you my word they will find both Nettie and Max to be healthy and as happy as we can make them. Look here comes Elmer now."

Kathleen spotted a sturdy framed man in his mid to late thirties, his face browned by the sun walking toward them. As he drew nearer, he swiped the hat from his head, his blue eyes full of concern, he looked more than a little bewildered. He played with his hat, passing it from one hand to the next as his eyes darted around the room, glancing at one child and then another. His eyes widened with relief when he spotted his wife. Pearl waved as he made his way from the entrance to where they stood near the front of the hall.

"Elmer, this is Mrs. Green, Bridget Watson's sister. She brought the children here. I already met Nettie, oh she is the prettiest little thing but so scared of me. I think I was too excitable."

"You?" Elmer joked before holding out his

hand to Kathleen. "Pleased to meet you Mrs. Green. I hope you had a pleasant journey."

"I did thank you. Your wife was just telling me about your talent for making toys, Mr. Haverford. You must have lots of energy as I imagine the farm keeps you busy."

"I do. It's hard work but good clean living. We have a small herd of cattle and some milk cows. Pearl has a vegetable garden and some hens for eggs, so we are fairly self-sufficient. We aren't rich but we have enough for us and for our new young'uns. Anything we need, we get from Riverside Springs. We rarely travel as far as Green River. But today is a special day."

"Would you expect the children to work on the farm?"

"Yes. Of course."

"Elmer!" Pearl flushed at his answer.

But he held Kathleen's gaze. "I would expect the children to help us and do their chores but it's not workers I want. We want to have a family. It's all we ever wanted and when God saw fit to take our boys home, well...we decided he had other plans for us. I give you my word, Mrs. Green, that we aim to treat the children we get as our own blood. They will go to school and learn their letters and get good grades. But they will also milk the cows, collect the eggs and as they get older help where needed. As long as I am fit and healthy, my family will not want for anything. Is that good enough?"

"Yes Mr. Haverford, for me. But it's not me you need to convince. Come and meet Max and Nettie."

She led the way over to the children. Nettie held Max's hand as her brother stared at the Haverfords, his face screwed up with distrust.

"Morning Max, Nettie. My name is Elmer and this here be my wife Pearl. Did you have a good journey on the train?'

Max's eyes darted from Kathleen to Elmer's and back again.

"Yes, sir."

"Good. Have you eaten this morning?"

"Yes, sir." Max stared at a point beyond Elmer's head. His tone wasn't rude but it couldn't be interpreted as friendly either.

Kathleen was tempted to intervene but something told her it would be better Elmer to handle the boy.

"Would you like to go find some ice-cream

if that was agreeable to Mrs. Green? Perhaps we could have a talk just the four of us and get to know one another a little bit. What do you say?"

Nettie jumped up and down. "Say yes Max. I never had ice-cream. It sounds nice."

Max quelled Nettie's exuberance with a glance. "Can we come back here to see Miss Kathleen?"

"Yes of course. We will just go down the town a little."

Max moved from one foot to the other. Kathleen spoke up. "Max, I will be here with the other children. You go on now and you can come back and tell me what you and Nettie thought of the ice-cream."

"Yes, Miss Kathleen but don't you go leaving on the train without us?"

"Do you think I would do that?" Kathleen held Max's gaze until he was the first to look away. She walked over to him and putting a hand on his shoulder, whispered into his ear. "They seem very nice to me, Max. Give them a chance. You can run back here if you get any bad feelings."

Max gave her a nod before stepping

forward. "We'd like to go and get some ice-cream please Mr. Haverford, sir."

Kathleen watched as the little group made their way out the back of the hall. She hoped that her good feeling about the Haverfords proved to be correct.

## CHAPTER 21

The day sped by, with several children matching with families who had written to Father Nelson or the Orphans Society. Kathleen kept a close eye on those signing for the children, but everything seemed in order. The Chiver children stayed together near the front of the hall, playing games or, as time passed, dozing in the seats, waiting until it was time to go home. While caught up in some paperwork, Kathleen heard a commotion from the back of the hall. She turned towards the noise and saw Mr. Forrester in a heated argument with two men. Excusing herself, she hurried to his side just as one man punched him in the nose, causing several women and children to scream as blood spurted from his face. Out of the corner of her eye, Kathleen caught sight of Miss Cooper rushing to his assistance.

*The children.* Despite her concern for Mr. Forrester, Kathleen knew her place was with them. She turned on her heel and hurried back to where she had last seen the Chiver children, only to find the seats empty. Panic surged through her until she spotted Max waving at her from across the hall, holding Nettie's hand, with Pearl Haverford holding onto the Chiver twins. Mr. Haverford had ordered several men in the hall to form a ring around the remaining children, clearly instructing them not to let anyone near. Kathleen quickly joined them.

"Thank you so much, Mr. Haverford. I don't know what's happening," she said.

"You stay here, Mrs. Green. The children need you. I'll check on your colleague," Mr. Haverford assured her, then marched towards the back of the hall.

"He's going to be my new Pa," Max whispered, watching Mr. Haverford catch one of the men by the shirt and escort him to the door, where the sheriff was waiting. The second man, the one who had punched Mr. Forrester, was already being escorted outside in handcuffs by a deputy.

The men spoke briefly before Mr. Forrester and Miss Cooper, escorted by Mr. Haverford, returned. Mr. Forrester's face was already swelling.

"What happened?" Kathleen asked, but he seemed unable to speak.

Miss Cooper, trembling, explained, "The men made some horrible remarks, and Mr. Forrester told them to mind their manners. They didn't like that, so they punched him."

"Those two men are no strangers to the jail-house. Nasty individuals who shouldn't have been allowed in here," Elmer Haverford commented. "The sheriff will deal with them. Still, you should see a doctor," he addressed Mr. Forrester, who shook his head but winced.

"I have my wagon out back. I can give you a ride to the hotel. Mrs. Klein will sort you out. She's nursed a few sore heads and faces in this town before. I'll come back for you and the rest of the children, Mrs. Green. You'll be safe here. The sheriff has left a deputy behind, but these good men won't let anyone near the children. I'm sure they've had enough for today."

"Thank you, Mr. Haverford. That would be lovely. Perhaps you could take Miss Cooper with you now, so she can get changed," Kathleen suggested.

Miss Cooper looked down at her blood-stained dress. "Oh dear, I don't look very smart now, do I?"

"You look like someone who rushed to rescue someone in distress. Go on with Mr. Haverford and ask Mrs. Klein for a glass of sweet tea for the shock," Kathleen reassured her.

"I'll wait here with you and the children," Pearl Haverford said, giving her husband a peck on the cheek before resuming her position beside Nettie. Kathleen was pleased to see the pair now holding hands.

Mr. Haverford returned, and they all traveled back to the hotel in his wagon. The children saw it as a wonderful adventure, joking and laughing, seemingly unperturbed by the events in the hall. Pearl insisted on sending Miss Cooper to bed and took her place helping the young girls get ready for bed, while Mr.

Haverford looked after the boys. Kathleen was grateful that the couple had decided to stay the night at the hotel. She listened outside the boys' bedroom as Mr. Haverford told a fantastical tale of good elves living in the woods, making presents for well-behaved children.

Hearing footsteps, Kathleen turned and saw Pearl, looking tired but happy.

"Is he telling the story about the Elves and the toys?" Pearl asked.

"Yes. He's very good with children," Kathleen replied, leading the way downstairs. "I wanted to thank both of you for your help, not just your husband's actions in the hall but with the bedtime routine. I wouldn't have managed without you."

"I think you would have, Mrs. Green, but if not, the Kleins would have helped. They told me about their children. They're so proud of them, and rightly so," Pearl responded.

Kathleen glanced at the photographs of the Klein children.

"How did you get on with Max and Nettie?" she asked.

Pearl's face lit up with a smile. "They're fantastic children, a bit wild around the edges, but that's to be expected, given what they've been through. You can tell their mother was a good woman with Christian values. I think they liked us too. Max and Elmer were talking about cattle and how Elmer is going to teach Max to ride a horse for the roundup next year, or maybe the year after when he's a bit older."

The thought of city-bred Max on a horse made Kathleen smile.

"They're very close, aren't they? The children, I mean," Pearl mused.

Kathleen closed her eyes, visualizing the scene outside the butcher's shop. "Yes. We had to force Nettie to come home with me after Max was hospitalized following the incident with the police."

Pearl clenched her hands. "I swear, if I had been there, I would have hit him with more than my handbag."

Kathleen blushed.

"Please don't be embarrassed. Nettie told us the story, complete with actions. She made us all laugh. She wasn't making fun of you; you're her hero," Pearl reassured her.

"Still, I could have handled that situation better," Kathleen admitted.

"But aren't you a little bit glad you gave that policeman a taste of his own medicine?" Pearl asked.

Kathleen glanced around, even though they were alone in the guest sitting room. "Yes. But I'll deny it if ever asked."

# CHAPTER 22

hat night, a cold wind brought a small flurry of snow, but by morning it had cleared. Kathleen was looking forward to reaching Riverside Springs and seeing her siblings. She dressed and packed quickly before rousing the children to go down for breakfast. Their train was leaving at midday.

Mr. Forrester made an appearance but didn't eat very much. The swelling on his face had turned multiple shades of black and purple, and he was obviously very embarrassed. He kept apologizing despite Kathleen, Miss Cooper, and the Haverfords telling him he hadn't done anything wrong.

Kathleen walked outside with Max and Nettie. Elmer and Pearl had gone ahead to give them privacy to say goodbye. Nettie hugged Kathleen. "Thank you, Miss Kathleen. I wish I didn't have to say goodbye to you, but I can't have you and my new parents."

"You can, darling. Mrs. Haverford said she will help you write to me. I can't wait to read all about your new life."

Nettie kept talking. "Pa is going to let me have a kitten. And a dog. But he won't be a house dog; he must stay in the shed. But I can feed him and look after him. He is going to get Max a horse. Do you think he will get me a horse when I am older like Max?"

"He probably will. Now, be a good girl and give me a last hug."

Max surprised her by giving her a hug as well. "Thank you for what you did for us, Miss Kathleen. They seem like nice people."

"They do, Max." She was troubled to see the distrust still lurking in his eyes.

"I got your address in my head; I learned it off. That way I can find you if I need to."

"You can, Max. I don't think you will need me. The Haverfords have said you will go to school in Riverside Springs. If you ever have any problem, talk to your schoolteacher. She is married to my brother. They will tell me."

Max's shoulders relaxed slightly.

"I know it's difficult for you to believe in people, Max. Give them a chance."

Max hugged her, and then without a word, got into the wagon, taking a seat in the back. Nettie sat up front between the Haverfords.

"Thank you, Mrs. Green. Maybe we will see you next Sunday if you are still in Riverside Springs. We won't be able to leave the farm tomorrow to get into the town, not with being away for the last two days."

Kathleen couldn't speak, her emotions threatening to overcome her. Saying goodbye to Nettie and Max was proving so difficult. She waved until they disappeared around a bend in the road.

The journey to Riverside Springs passed quickly, with the children asking lots of questions about what type of animals they were likely to see. Hearing about Max getting a horse had made the Chiver boys wonder if they too would be so lucky. Kathleen wasn't sure what animals the orphanage kept, if any, so she kept silent. Miss Cooper chatted with the children, but Kathleen sensed the curious looks she sent her way. Finally, the younger woman whispered, "Are you all right, Mrs. Green? You look very sad."

"I'm fine. It was just harder to say goodbye than I thought it would be."

Miss Cooper squeezed her hand in support before she answered the children's question about whether it was true they had to attend school every day.

"Not every day. They give you Sunday off so you can attend church."

The children groaned, making Kathleen smile. She stared out the window, wondering if she would recognize her friend Bella now after all these years. They had met at the sanctuary before Bella had come west and settled in Riverside Springs, marrying the man who had written for a bride. The man Bridget was supposed to marry until she fell in love with Carl Watson. Kathleen hoped her sister had listened to the advice of her doctors and was taking things easier. Although knowing Bridget, that was unlikely.

As the train pulled into the town, they

heard singing. "Is there a party on today, Miss Kathleen?" Carrie Chiver poked Kathleen in the arm when she didn't answer, her gaze stuck on the vision standing on the platform. There was Bridget and her husband and children, Shane standing with his arm around Angel, their children standing in front of them. Other children swarmed the platform along with the twins, Megan and Eileen Doyle. Tears ran down Kathleen's face.

"Why is Miss Kathleen crying, Miss Cooper?"

"I'm crying because I'm happy, Carrie. That's my sister and my brother, and that lady is my friend Bella. And the lady wearing the blue hat is Megan, standing beside her sister Eileen. They came here on an orphan train years ago. Some of those children did too. And now they are all here to greet us. It's so sweet of them."

"Do you think they will have chocolate cake?" Carrie rubbed her stomach.

"You never think of anything but your stomach, Carrie."

Carrie stuck her tongue out at her brothers,

but for once, Kathleen didn't correct her. She was far too overcome with emotion. She couldn't wait for the train doors to open.

Even the conductor on the train seemed to know about the party arranged to welcome them to Riverside Springs. Kathleen stood, surrounded by family and friends, blocking the platform. Everyone spoke at once until Shane put his fingers together and whistled.

"Give Kathleen a chance to catch her breath, and let's get these children off the platform and safely into Riverside Springs. We wouldn't want the train to be late and get Mr. Grange into trouble with the railroad."

The conductor nodded his thanks.

Kathleen checked that all the children had left the train and watched them walking out of the station and into Riverside Springs, escorted by members of her family. Bridget hung back to walk at Kathleen's side.

"I'm so glad to see you. I never thought you would leave New York and visit us. Next time, you will have to bring Richard and the children."

Kathleen clutched her sister's arm, not

wanting to admit even to herself the scare she'd got on seeing her. Bridget didn't look well and looked much older than her thirty-eight years. She was too thin for a start, and her skin around her mouth had a bluish tinge to it.

"I hope you are resting like the doctor ordered."

Bridget didn't answer, but her smile turned mutinous, making Kathleen laugh.

"That's the same look you had on your face when we were fired by Mr. Oaks. Do you remember him?" Kathleen matched her steps to her sister, who walked slowly.

"How could we ever forget?" Bridget seemed to find it hard to speak and walk at the same time. She stopped for a second. "I guess we should thank him. I'd never have met Carl or you, Richard, had we stayed working in his factory."

That was true. Funny how something horrible had set them on a road to such fulfilling lives. They wouldn't have met Lily or got involved with the orphan train.

"Where are we going now? To your house?"

"No, to the orphanage. You can't get cross

with me. The girls insisted on a party, but they also made sure I didn't do any of the work. They wanted to do something special for you and the Chiver children. And the other children you brought with you, although we expected more."

"We matched more children with parents in Green Rivers. The Kleins advocated on behalf of the children. I think if they were a little younger, they would have adopted another two children themselves. They are such a lovely couple and so proud of their two."

"They have reason to be. Life hasn't been easy for them, but they made that hotel work and put those children through years of schooling. Their lives have turned out totally different than if they had remained living in the squalor of the New York tenements."

Bridget lapsed into silence for the rest of the walk. Kathleen looked around the town with interest, at the store where Bella had first stayed before she married Brian Curran. When they reached the orphanage, Kathleen insisted Bridget return to her home to rest for a while.

"I will catch up with you properly this

evening, but first you must rest. Kenny said your doctors had told you that. I will get straight back on the train and return to New York if you don't do as you are told."

For a brief second, Kathleen thought her sister would tell her off, but instead, she nodded. "You never used to be so bossy, Kathleen. I am feeling a little drained. There are loads of people who want to speak to you, so I will take your advice and rest."

"Good." Kathleen kissed her sister's cheek and watched as Bridget followed the path behind the orphanage to her home. The door to the orphanage opened about the same time as Bridget's front door shut behind her. Kathleen was swept into a hug from Bella Curran.

"I can't believe you are really here after all this time. You look wonderful." Bella held Kathleen at arm's length, her eyes roving over her outfit. "You are dressed to perfection; that color matches your eyes. You are very much a lady about town now."

"I'm still the same old me. You look wonderful; Riverside Springs really agrees with you." Kathleen couldn't believe the change in her old friend. Bella had been the victim of hideous abuse from the people who'd adopted her from an orphan train. But she'd turned her life around when she'd met Lily at the sanctuary and then agreed to come to Wyoming. "This has changed a lot, hasn't it? Do you remember the first letter you wrote to me saying that this place wasn't even big enough to be called a town. It barely had a road, a store, and a church. And now look at it."

Bella glanced around at the wooden-fronted buildings on the main street as if seeing things for the first time. "I suppose it has changed a lot. There are more stores, blacksmiths, machinery repair stores, and of course, restaurants and my dress shop."

"I'm looking forward to seeing that. After reading your letters, I feel like I know it already. You must be very proud of your success."

Bella shrugged. "I was, but it's a bit difficult now. A lot of people are buying from those magazine catalogues. The mass-produced clothes are a lot cheaper than anything I can make. But we get by. Brian has built up the farm, and the children are all happy and healthy. We have a lot to be thankful for. I'm sorry, though, that I couldn't offer your friend Leonie a full-time job. Do you think she will still come to Riverside Springs?"

"Yes, she won't want to be separated from her siblings. She feels responsible for them and was reluctant for them to travel here without her. But she needs a lot of treatments and rest before she will be able to walk again."

"You believe she will? Walk, I mean? Kenny spoke about how tiring it is for her."

Kathleen caught the curiosity in Bella's eyes. Her old friend hadn't changed that much.

"Richard always thought it was a reaction to the trauma she suffered rather than there being a physical cause, so we keep our fingers crossed." Kathleen glanced behind Bella at the noise coming from the orphanage.

"I'm sorry, I'm monopolizing you out here when so many are waiting to greet you inside. We should head in."

"Wait, Bella. There is something I need to ask you. Bridget didn't look very well. Did I catch her at a bad time, or is she always like this?"

Bella glanced in the direction of Bridget's home. "We are worried about her. She won't slow down. There was some trouble out at the mines, some children were injured, and Bridget wanted to go out and meet with the owners. Thankfully, Carl put his foot down, but you know your sister. She isn't one for being told what to do. She may be older, but she hasn't got any wiser."

"Kathleen Green, are you going to come in and say hello, or will you make this old woman come out to you?"

Kathleen glanced up, shocked to see Mrs. Grayson leaning heavily on a cane on the steps to the orphanage. She hurried towards the old woman.

"You shouldn't be out here. Let's get you back inside and sitting down," Kathleen urged.

"Stop fussing," Mrs. Grayson protested, but even as she spoke, she allowed Kathleen to help her into the orphanage. Together, they found some chairs. Kathleen listened intently as the old woman brought her up to date on her family and friends. It seemed there was nothing that escaped Mrs. Grayson's notice. As Kathleen absorbed the stories of all that the children had accomplished, she found herself wishing Lily were here to see their achievements. Despite some terrible incidents over the years, with children being placed in bad homes and suffering as a result, the children sent from New York had thrived in this lovely town. Kathleen hoped this would continue.

# CHAPTER 23

*L*ily had just finished her breakfast in the kitchen when Maeve came back in, her face white. "Have you seen the newspapers? My word, what a lucky escape you and Charlie had. If he hadn't hurt his ankle, you would have been on board, and knowing your husband, he would have stepped aside and made sure the women and children got off first. He would have been lost."

"Maeve, calm down. I can't make sense of what you are saying. You're speaking too fast. What's wrong?"

The woman held out the newspaper. Lily's eyes froze on the headline,

*Titanic Sinks after Collision*

"Oh my word, how? What did it collide with? The ocean is huge, it couldn't have been another boat. They would have seen each other. But it was supposed to be unsinkable? Is everyone dead? Surely not." Lily babbled as she struggled to take the news in.

Maeve did what she always did in a crisis and made some tea. Lily read out the coverage from the newspaper.

"It says here several passengers were picked up by another ship, the Carpathia. They will print the names of those saved soon. Oh Maeve, there are a few children among the missing, feared dead. Most were traveling in second and third class."

"God have pity on their souls," Maeve made the sign of the cross. Then she did it again. "Thank the good Lord you and Charlie had to stay here. I couldn't have borne reading about a tragedy like that knowing you were in danger. I've grown fond of the pair of you since you arrived."

Lily could see Maeve's lips moving, but she couldn't hear what she was saying. The noise in her head grew louder. If Charlie hadn't hurt his leg, they would have been on that ship when it sank in the middle of the freezing Atlantic. Her children would have been orphans. The band tightened around her heart, making it difficult to breathe. She could see her boys, Laurie and Teddy, trying to be brave for the girls. She wanted nothing more than to touch them, to reassure them.

"Lily, Lily," Maeve's voice pierced the fog. "Lily."

She focused on the old woman now looking at her in fright. "I thought you were going to pass out; you lost all color in your cheeks. You poor darling, you must be so scared. It doesn't bear thinking about. I think you should go for a nap. Go on up and hold your husband close."

"What about Paddy?"

"Who?"

"Niamh mentioned a boy called Paddy. They were to have an American wake for him the Saturday after Charlie's fall. He was due to travel to America on the Titanic."

"I don't know who you mean, but Frank will. I'll ask him when I see him. Now away you go to bed. Go on. I know you haven't been sleeping much the last few days, but if ever you needed proof that God didn't want you to travel, this is it."

Lily climbed the stairs slowly, each step taking a huge effort. How had they been so lucky? She let a bitter laugh escape. Who'd have thought breaking your ankle would be considered lucky. She stopped at the top of the stairs, standing outside their bedroom. The newspaper article had said women and children had been saved first. Even if there was a slim chance, she would have survived the sinking, it seemed that most of the men had gone down with the ship. How close she had come to losing Charlie?

She shivered. That was one loss she couldn't bear, and it had taken this trip to Ireland to remind her of how much she loved her husband. She had let Carmel's Mission dominate her life, taking up time that she should have spent with her own children and her husband. What type of woman was she? Things would change when she got back to New York. From now on, her husband and her children were her priorities. It was time to put them first.

She pushed the door open, but the creak it made woke Charlie. He gave her a sleepy half-smile.

"How are you? Is the pain bad? Do you need something?"

"A drink of water would be good. I must have been snoring; my throat is so… Lily, what is it? Why are you crying?"

"I love you, Charlie, you have no idea how much. I really love you."

"I love you too. What's brought this on?" He winced as he pulled himself to a seating position in the bed. "Come here and sit down."

She went to the bed, trying not to hurt him when she sat down.

"I've missed you lying beside me. I know Maeve thinks I will recover quicker sleeping alone, but I think she's wrong. I don't like you being gone."

"Oh, Charlie," Lily couldn't help it; the tears flooded down her cheeks as she sobbed on his shoulder. He rubbed her back, letting her cry.

"Lily, tell me. Did something happen to the children?"

She shook her head.

"Kathleen, Richard? Someone we know?"

"The Titanic. It sank, Charlie, and lots of passengers are missing. That could have been us."

"What? But it couldn't have."

"Yet it did."

Lily cried as she read the newspaper articles out to him, the stories of those who survived and those who drowned.

"Most of those who died were men, Charlie. Even when the lifeboats weren't full, they didn't let the men get in. If we... if you hadn't had your accident, I could have lost you. Our children could have lost both of us."

"I know, Lily. We were lucky."

"I couldn't bear it if I lost you, Charlie. Regardless of what you think, you and the children are my life."

"Lily, I'm sorry. I didn't mean all those things I said to you the other night."

"Yes, you did. You're right too. I have been distracted, sad, and overwhelmed. It isn't like the old days, Charlie. Back then, I thought I was making a difference. But now, I just feel for every woman or child we rescue, there are ten or more lining up to take their place. It's never-ending. Until we came here, I couldn't sleep, and I know I was difficult to live with."

He didn't say anything.

"You could be a gentleman and tell me I was a wonderful wife."

He smiled. "I came close to dying; now is not the time to take up lying."

She slapped him gently on his good arm.

"I love you, Lily. I can't say the last few months haven't been challenging, but you are not the only one at fault. I should have spoken up sooner. I could see you were struggling, but I'm so used to you being so strong." He turned to reach for the water, but she beat him to it. She filled a glass and handed it to him, watching him take a long drink.

"I think you are wrong; every single person you and the sanctuary have helped is an achievement. But it is different. Maybe the time has come for you to pass the baton to someone else. You could stay home and take up knitting." He grinned to show her he was joking, but she sensed he was also serious.

"I could try. I've never sat at home all day doing nothing. I'm not sure I'm built that way."

"Nobody is saying you must sit around, but

just cut back on the work you are doing. You can still fundraise or help in some way but leave the day-to-day running of Carmel's Mission to someone else. Kathleen? Maybe not, as she has been working as long as you. What about Emily? You said yourself she was capable and loved working there."

Emily. That was a good idea but what of the school she had started. Maybe she could move the school to the sanctuary, it was close enough. Gustav would be on hand to help her, just like Charlie had helped in the early days.

"Couldn't you give it a try?" Charlie's tentative tone gave her a lump in her throat.

"Charlie, I can do more than try. I love you so much and can't bear the thought of you thinking I don't. This accident, the Titanic sinking, being here in Ireland, all of it has made me think. I'm giving up all my work. From now on, our family comes first."


LATE THE NEXT DAY, hearing voices she knocked on the kitchen door to find Frank and Maeve. Both were nursing a glass of whiskey.

"I'm sorry, would you rather be alone?"

"No Lily, come in and sit down. I'll pour you a glass."

"I'll have water but thank you." Lily sat down at the table.

"That poor boy you were asking for, Paddy. Seems he died on the ship. His mammy got a telegram this morning from her other son in New York. Waiting for the ship he was. Tis an awful business." Maeve took a sip of her whiskey.

Frank raised his glass. "Thank God you weren't on the ship too Lily. We think of you and Charlie as family now, don't we?"

"We do, so we do." Maeve clinked glasses before having another sip. Then she stood up. "I best get the dinner sorted. Can't be sitting around all day."

Lily stood up. "Let me help. I'm not much of a cook but even I can't ruin potatoes."

# CHAPTER 24

"Mrs. Green, I mean Kathleen, could I have a word with you?" Miss Cooper said as she walked into the room, her face pale but her chin set in a determined fashion.

"Of course, Lisa. You sound very serious. Is everything alright?"

"I am very grateful to you for trusting me and engaging my services as an agent on the Orphan Train. But…" Lisa looked up and then looked away, but not before Kathleen saw her lip tremble. She was nervous, poor thing.

"But?"

"I wondered if I might stay in Riverside Springs rather than return with you to New

York. Mrs. Watson has so many orphans to look after. I could help, and I won't cost very much. I don't expect to be paid other than a small amount to cover my food and lodgings. I love working with children, but not when they are sick like in the hospital. I think I could help Mrs. Watson and... Oh, I am running on, aren't I? Matron always said I spoke too much. I forget myself."

"Ignore everything Matron said to you, my dear girl. If anyone was ever born to work with children, you would be that person. You have endless patience yet also know when to be firm with the children who could take advantage. I believe you would be an asset to the orphanage."

"You do?"

The doubt in her voice made Kathleen mad. It wasn't Miss Cooper's fault, but those who believed an orphan was less than a human being. Kathleen wished she could scrub away all the unkind things this girl had been subjected to over the years.

"Yes, I do. What's more, so does Mr. Watson and several of the board members who oversee this orphanage. Bridget may have set it up, but with the way it has expanded, there is now a board in charge. They will have to give you a formal offer, but now we know you would like to stay here, I will ask them to organize that."

Miss Cooper clapped her hands, her smile reaching her eyes. "Thank you, Mrs. Green, I mean Kathleen. I don't think I will ever get used to calling you by your Christian name."

"Well, you should, Lisa. We are equals, you and I. Now, about your salary…"

The girl opened her mouth, but Kathleen ignored her.

"You will receive a small salary every month. My husband insists, and he will fund it. As you know, the orphanage is in dire need of funds, so they can't spare any extra money at this time. If you wish to move in, that would be helpful as it means Bridget can stop her overnight stays. My sister is starting to see reason – well, she may just be saying things to keep me happy. But she knows she must reduce her workload. If you live here with the children, she can stay home more and rest. At least that's the plan."

"I'd love to live here. It's such a beautiful home. Not just a building with walls and a roof, but a real home. The children are happy here. I want to help keep it that way."

Kathleen gave the girl a warm hug. "You are a lovely young lady, Lisa, and never let anyone tell you otherwise. In time, I'm sure a young man will come along and sweep you off your feet." Kathleen glanced out the window to the street outside. When the orphanage was built, it was set a little way outside of town, but with the town expansion, they were now in quite a busy area. Thankfully, Bridget and the others had secured a large field behind the orphanage so that it could expand when the funds became available.

"I don't think that will happen to me."

Kathleen turned back to the young woman. "If I had a dollar for every time I heard that before, I wouldn't need much funding for this place." They both laughed. "There are so many single men in Wyoming; you will be spoiled for choice. I just ask that you take your time to pick the right man. You deserve to be happy."

"I have plenty of time to think about all that when I am older. Today, I have some white-washing to do. Mr. Larsen, the new owner of the Grayson store, was having a clear-out and donated some. People in this town are so generous, aren't they?"

"Yes, they are." Kathleen agreed. "It's rather a special place, but then I think I am related to half the residents in some way, so I might be biased."

Later that day, Kathleen found Bridget in the orphanage office.

"I haven't even left yet, and here you are breaking your promise to rest more."

Bridget flushed guiltily. "I'm just sorting out some paperwork. It isn't fair to hand over a mess to Miss Cooper."

Kathleen glanced at the files. "I'm sure the systems you use will be easy for Lisa to pick up. Come on, walk with me. I have to pack for my return trip tomorrow."

They walked arm in arm from the Orphanage to Bridget's home.

"I've enjoyed these few days more than words can say, Kathleen. Do you think you could come to Riverside Springs more often?"

"Yes. I'm going to bring Esme and Richie to visit in the summer. New York becomes unbearable in the heat."

"Charming! You are running away from the

seasonal temperatures rather than looking forward to seeing your family." Bridget teased, her smile matching Kathleen's. Kathleen gave her an impulsive hug. "I love you, Bridget, and miss you. The last few days have shown me how much. Meeting all my nieces and nephews, seeing Bella and her family, Megan, and Eileen. I don't want to let more years pass without building relationships between my children and their cousins. So, I think you might get sick of me."

"Never."

"When I get back to New York, I will work harder on the fundraising for the orphanage. When I met those young boys from the mines, their stories broke my heart. How can people be so cruel?"

"Their parents need the money they earn to keep the family alive. The fault lies with the mine owners who don't put the proper safety precautions in place and who insist on employing children despite knowing the dangers."

Kathleen put a finger to her lips. "Shush now, you will get your heart racing if you get all agitated on me. Can you write to me, outlining the problems you see in the mines? Maybe Charlie can speak to someone who has power to make changes. He has to know someone and if he doesn't, Lily's old friend Mr. Prentice will."

"I bet you can't wait to see Lily and Charlie again."

Kathleen crossed herself. "When I think of how close we came to losing them. I know it's a horrible thing to say, but I'm so glad they missed the sailing of the Titanic. I feel so sorry for all those who died, but I don't think I could bear it to lose Lily."

"She is like a sister to us, isn't she?"

"She is part of my family. Without her, I shudder to think what our lives would have turned out like." Kathleen hesitated, not wanting to upset Bridget. But she had to know.

"Do you ever wonder where Maura is? It's hard to believe it's been almost twenty years since she ran away."

Bridget shook her head. "Maura was a grown woman and she made her own choices. I know that sounds harsh, but she wasn't interested in helping her family when she could. I hope life turned out well for her, but I don't waste too much time thinking about it."

"Bridget! It's been so long, surely it's time to forgive her."

"It's not my place to forgive her; that's between her and God. I just can't forget that she stole from Lily and hurt Bella in the process."

Kathleen wished she'd never mentioned their older sister.

"Kathleen, I'm sorry. You didn't know Maura as well as I did. She was selfish through to her core. The opposite of you. When I think of how determined you were to find Shane and Michael. If it hadn't been for you, we wouldn't have Shane, Angel, and their beautiful children in our lives. Let's concentrate on those who we love and love us in return."

Bridget gave her a hug, and Kathleen took the hint. The subject of Maura was closed as far as Bridget was concerned.

# CHAPTER 25

*N*iamh and Tom were frequent visitors to see Charlie.

Frank was excited about the chance to get into business with the two boys as he called them. Maeve also wanted to invest some money.

"I might as well. I have no children to leave it too and I can't bring it with me when I die."

Lily hid a smile as Frank and Maeve started arguing about who should do what and when. Frank escaped by going to Dublin with Tom to fetch Declan home. The boy was happy to be going into business as a cattle dealer and Frank had found a friend who would show him the ropes.

Lily sat at the table one evening with Niamh. "I've been thinking of your lace work. My friend got married at Christmas and everyone commented on her lovely lace veil. If you could make a few of those, we could sell them in New York for you. They would make you a few dollars for yourself." Lily coloured. "Not that I mean you should keep money from Tom but I thought you might feel a bit more secure if you had a little nest egg of your own. Maybe if Louise were to help you, she could give up her job and then take up a teaching training position when one came available. What do you think?"

Niamh hugged her, tears in her eyes. "I think it's a lucky day you crossed my threshold. You have turned our lives around."

"You have helped me more than you know too. Did Charlie tell you we are coming back to Ireland in late summer with our children. I can't wait for them to meet all their cousins."

"And me, I hope!"

Maeve put her arms around Lily.

"Of course." Lily had grown very fond of the old woman who'd done more than anyone could have asked.

. . .

WHEN IT CAME time to leave, there were more tears but with promises to return, Charlie and Lily boarded the train. They waved out the window until their Irish family had long disappeared from view. Sitting back in their seats, Charlie held Lily's hand. "Are you sure this is what you want?"

"Absolutely. I can't wait to bring the children back here to see this beautiful place. Maybe we could convince your mother and grandmother to come too."

Charlie chuckled. "I'd love to be a fly on the wall when Carmel hears Frank said she was his girl."

Lily lay her head against her husband's shoulder thinking how lucky they were.

# CHAPTER 26

*L*ily pushed open the door to the office, watching Kathleen in silence for a few minutes. Her best friend, closer than a sister, had her head down, concentrating on the paperwork in front of her. Lily hesitated, starting to second-guess her decision. Would Kathleen feel betrayed?

"Are you going to come in and sit down, or just stand there letting all the heat out?" Kathleen put the papers to one side and sat back in her chair.

Lily came in, closing the door behind her. She had asked Ethel to ensure they weren't disturbed.

"Come and sit by me on the couch."

"What's wrong? Are you ill? The children? Why do you look so serious?"

"Stop fussing, Kathleen, and sit down. I want to talk to you about something."

Lily wiped her clammy hands on her skirt, wondering if the room was too hot or if it was just her nerves. She opened her mouth, but her throat was too dry to speak. This was more difficult than she had believed.

"Are you trying to tell me you're leaving the sanctuary?" Kathleen prompted.

Shocked, Lily could only stare. It took her several seconds to find her voice. "How did you know?"

"I knew something happened in Ireland. At first, I thought it was a reaction to you missing the Titanic and feeling guilty about surviving."

Lily gulped as Kathleen described exactly how she had been feeling.

"You know me so well."

"Lily, you are like a sister to me. You mean more really as we can't choose our family, but we can choose our friends. You have given everything you had to this place and to helping everyone who needed you, but now you have to do what is right for you."

"Have you been reading tea leaves? How can you know all that?"

Kathleen grinned. "Charlie may have given the game away. Not that he meant to, but I overheard him talking to Grace about taking her to meet her cousins in Ireland. He said he has some business deal he wants to set up involving cows?" Kathleen looked confused.

Lily smiled. "Cattle. Charlie and his cousin Tom are going into the cattle dealing business together. There's a market here for Irish cattle. And it means Charlie will get to spend more time in Ireland. I want to be with him. I owe him... No, it's more than that. I love him and I want to spend more time with him. My priorities over the years haven't always put my own family first, and it's time that changed." Lily's heart was racing. She hated hurting Kathleen. "I don't mean I regret anything I did. I've loved being here, working alongside you and the others. But..."

"Lily, you don't need to explain anything. I feel the same. Well, not about becoming a cattle dealer, but the rest." Kathleen smiled, despite the tears shining in her eyes. "I loved the days I spent in Riverside Springs, catching up with my family, our friends, the orphans we rescued. We did all those things together. I will always be grateful to you, Lily, for what you did not just for the Collins family but for giving me a purpose. But, like you, I want to spend more time with my family. I want to give Esme and Richie a chance to build the bonds with their cousins that I have with my siblings."

Lily put her hand in her pocket, looking for a handkerchief. Kathleen handed hers over.

"I was so worried about talking to you. I didn't want you thinking I was tired of you."

"I'd never think that. Well, maybe after an argument or two." Kathleen smiled at her, taking her hand and squeezing it. "You are stuck with me, Lily Doherty. And who knows, maybe one day I will cross the ocean with you and visit the home of my family."

"Dublin was where your parents lived, wasn't it? It's such a wonderful city, but there is so much poverty. You should see the tenements the people live in…" Lily stopped as Kathleen laughed.

"What?"

"You might say you are giving up working for a living, but something tells me you will have a new cause to fight for if you do move to Ireland."

Lily couldn't disagree. There were lots of things she would want to change in Ireland. The first one being that the land belonged to those farmers who toiled so hard on it. She also believed Ireland belonged to the Irish.

They sat in companionable silence for a few minutes. Kathleen was the first to speak. "So when will we ask Emily and Gustav if they are ready to move in and look after this place?"

Lily shouldn't have been surprised when Kathleen put her own idea into words.

"You do agree, don't you? Emily is perfect; she knows the routines and is wonderful with the women. Gustav is handy around the place; he can repair almost anything. Also, he provides some security, which is never a bad thing given some of the situations the women who end up here come from. They won't have much involvement with the official orphan trains as Father Nelson said things were changing. The Catholic Church is running their own trains, and the Orphan Society has their way of dealing with things. In fact, the board at both those institutions may throw a party when they hear Lily Doherty is retiring."

Lily stuck out her tongue in a very unlady-like way. "If you think they like you any more than me, you are much mistaken. At least I don't go around beating up policemen with handbags!"

"I'm never going to live that one down, am I? Oh, that reminds me, Inspector Griffin is retiring. Did he tell you? His wife has put her foot down and told him enough is enough. She wants to leave the city and find a small holding to raise a few hens and grow her own vegetables."

Lily couldn't help herself. "Did you suggest they go to Riverside Springs and settle there?"

Kathleen flushed a little. "I might have." She shrugged. "I like keeping my friends close. Inspector Griffin is part of our family now. Whether he likes it or not."

"I think he likes it."

Kathleen stood up. "I'm going to ask Cook for a cup of tea. Talking about the future is thirsty work."

"I wonder what she will do when we tell her? Do you think she will want to leave?"

Kathleen shook her head. "Not immediately, although she isn't getting any younger. But she likes Emily, and she loves looking after all the women who end up here. She'd have been a wonderful mother, wouldn't she?"

Lily nodded as Kathleen left the room and came back in a few minutes. "Ethel will bring the tea in when it's ready." Kathleen sat down again. "What about the factory?"

"We will need to have a meeting with Mr. Prentice and the other shareholders, but I'm going to propose that Gustav and Conrad be promoted. Conrad can run the day-to-day things; he's younger and more open to new developments. Gustav can remain in charge of recruitment and personnel."

"And the fire drills."

Lily smiled. She'd heard no end of moaning from the staff over the fire drills Gustav insisted on, but she believed he was correct. They could never be too prepared.

# EPILOGUE

wo weeks later, at the official opening of the factory, Lily watched their friends enjoying the party. She giggled at Richard and Kathleen attempting the Grizzly Bear and the Turkey Trot; they were braver than she was. Drinks flowed, while colorful streamers and paper lanterns hung from the ceilings and walls, adding to the festive appearance. Sounds of laughter and lively chatter filled the room as their family, friends, and close associates came together to celebrate. Children scampered about, their faces smeared with chocolate cake or ice cream, chasing each other and giggling, their parents smiling at their antics. Granny Belbin,

Cook, and a few other older folks sat together, no doubt reminiscing about the old days. Nobody cared that the opening celebration was almost six months late, knowing the delay was partly due to Charlie's good fortune in breaking his ankle and thus being saved from the awful fate of the Titanic passengers. Nor did it bother them that some party guests, like Mr. Prentice and Anne Morgan, were among the richest people living in America, while others were among the poorest. Everyone was dressed in their best, thanks in no small part to the efforts of Leonie, Emily, and the other staff at the Sanctuary, who had provided new dresses to those unable to afford them.

LILY WATCHED AS KENNY, back on leave, waltzed Leonie around the dance floor, despite the band playing a rousing Charleston number. The romance, while still in its early days, was thriving, and tomorrow Kenny would accompany Leonie to Riverside Springs. Her treatments were at an end; she could walk but needed one crutch for more than just crossing a room. In time, she might be able to do without it, but compared to being in a wheel-chair, she was happy. The adoring look on Kenny's face when he looked at Leonie brought a lump to Lily's throat. She took a hasty sip of champagne, rehearsing the words of her speech in her head, terrified she was going to make a fool of herself.

"Are you ready, darling?" Charlie whispered in her ear before planting a quick kiss on her earlobe.

She nodded, even though her dinner was threatening to make a reappearance. Charlie's limp was more pronounced that evening as he accompanied her to the front of the room, squeezing her hand as everyone clapped when they realized she intended to make a speech. Charlie motioned to the band to stop playing, as he released her and stepped to the side, leaving her standing alone in front of all their family, friends, and guests.

"Thank you, everyone, for coming here tonight and for your patience at this long-awaited opening. I'm pleased to announce the factory is growing from strength to strength under the guidance of Conrad and Gustav. Please give them a round of applause for their hard work." Lily gestured at Conrad and Gustav to join her. Neither of them was comfortable in the spotlight, but she insisted.

"We have a surprise to announce this evening. With the agreement of Mr. Prentice and Miss Anne Morgan, both Conrad and Gustav have been promoted and will now be responsible for all issues relating to the factory, including the fire drills."

Her comment drew laughter, groans, and whistles. Gustav took it in good faith, bowing to the crowd.

When the crowd quieted down, Lily gestured to Kathleen to join her.

"As most of you know, we set up Carmel's Mission after seeing the effects of the horrible blizzard back in 1888. We envisioned a small sanctuary for those women and children whom life had mistreated. In that time, thanks in large part to many of you here, we have thrived and supported more people than we ever thought possible. Carmel's Mission will continue to be a place of sanctuary in New York for as long as it is needed." Lily stopped talking, waiting for the clapping to die down. She saw the curious looks her guests were exchanging. This was it. Once she made this public, there was no going back. She glanced at Kathleen, who gave her a small nod of encouragement.

Lily coughed, trying to keep her voice steady. "Kathleen Collins arrived at the sanctuary almost twenty years ago as a young and, you will never guess, fairly timid woman."

"She didn't stay that way for long." Inspector Griffin's voice carried more than he intended, judging by his red cheeks, but his comment drew more laughter. Lily smiled before continuing, "Her character grew in response to the many challenges she faced, helping those members of society that need it most. She became my trusted friend, my ally, and my family. Please raise a glass to her health."

The shouts of "Kathleen" grew around the room. Kathleen turned several shades of red before Lily raised a hand, asking for quiet.

"The time has come for Kathleen and me to step back from our roles in the sanctuary." The room fell silent as people glanced at one another. "Emily has very graciously agreed to take over and from this evening is now in charge of Carmel's Mission. Congratulations, Emily, and thank you."

Emily took a quick bow but didn't move from her husband's side.

Before Lily could continue, Kathleen spoke up.

"You've talked enough, Lily; it's my turn now." Everyone laughed, as Kathleen no doubt intended.

Kathleen turned to Lily and raised her glass. "To the woman who started it all, to the lives she changed, to those she saved, and to those she couldn't. May we remember all of them."

The crowd clapped, but Kathleen motioned for them to be quiet. "We all know that Lily Doherty is a force to be reckoned with. She tells me she is retiring to live quietly as Charlie's wife and mother to his children. I'm sure that is her intention... for now." Everyone laughed again. Lily squirmed, wondering what her friend would say next.

"It doesn't take spending twenty years with someone as fantastic as Lily Doherty to know that despite her best intentions, she will be right in the heart of things if she ever finds someone in trouble. That's just who she is, and it's one of the many reasons we all love her so much. To Lily Doherty. May she and Charlie have the future they deserve, surrounded by loved ones and some very healthy cattle."

Everyone cheered and clapped as Kathleen kissed Lily's cheek, and then Charlie swung her up in his arms and kissed her like a groom kisses his bride on their wedding day.

# AFTERWORD

Thank you so much for reading
my books and spending time with
Lily, Kathleen and their friends at
Carmel's Mission.

I have the most amazing readers
in the world and am very grateful to
each and every one of you. I love
your emails and your comments in the
Facebook group. If you have yet to
join please do visit at https://www.
facebook.com/groups/rachelwesson
sreaders.

If you would like to join my
email list, please do :-) I promise

I won't spam you or pass your email to anyone else. If you click this link, https://dl.bookfunnel.com/vn-b9qauju9 and you will also get a free book.

Thank you all again.

Rachel x

ALSO BY RACHEL WESSON

**The Resistance Sisters**

Darkness Falls

Light Rises

**Hearts at War**

When's Mummy Coming

A Mother's Promise

**WWII Irish Stand Alone**

Stolen from her Mother

**Orphans of Hope House**

Home for unloved Orphans (Orphans of Hope
House 1)

Baby on the Doorstep (Orphans of Hope House 2)

**Women and War**

Gracie under Fire

Penny's Secret Mission

Molly's Flight

**Hearts on the Rails**

Orphan Train Escape

Orphan Train Trials

Orphan Train Christmas

Orphan Train Tragedy

Orphan Train Strike

Orphan Train Disaster

Orphan Train Memories


**Trail of Hearts - Oregon Trail Series**

Oregon Bound (book 1)

Oregon Dreams (book 2)

Oregon Destiny (book 3)

Oregon Discovery (book 4)

Oregon Disaster (book 5)


**12 Days of Christmas - co -authored series.**

The Maid - book 8


**Clover Springs Mail Order Brides**

Katie (Book 1)

Mary (Book 2)

Sorcha (Book 3)

Printed in Great Britain
by Amazon

42274447R00179